Circle to Paris

Honora Favre Romance Series
Book 1

LINDA F. BARRETT

To my darling husband, John

who has held my hand throughout the journey of writing this book and always encouraged me to live, love, and create.

Table of Contents

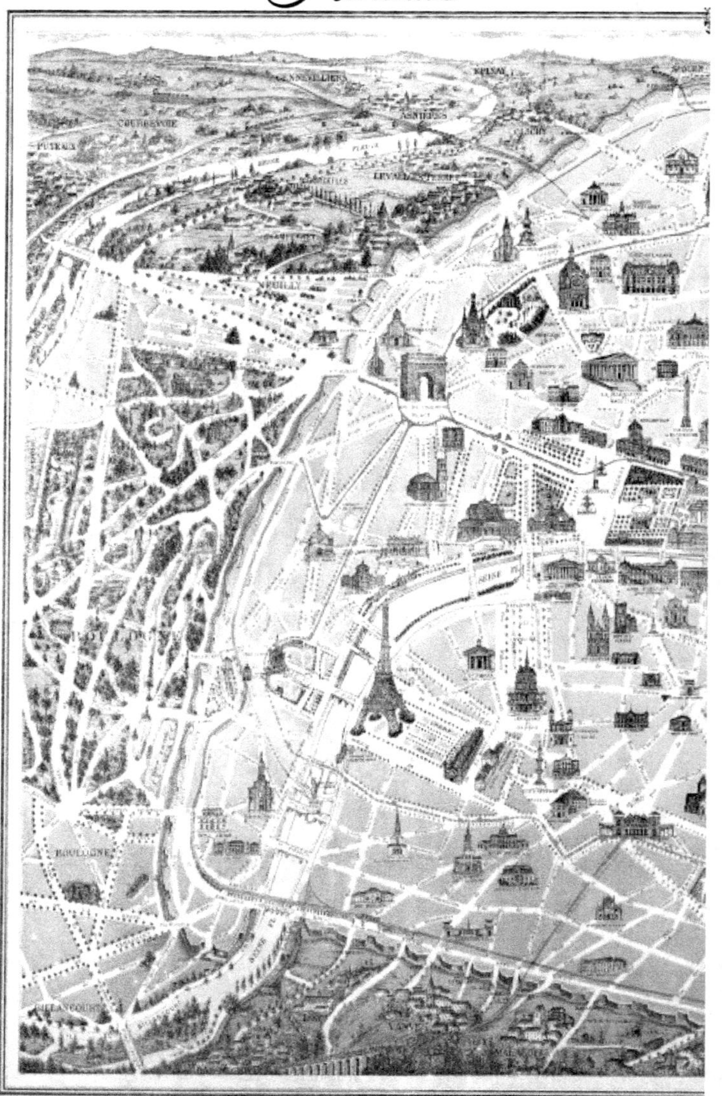

Paris

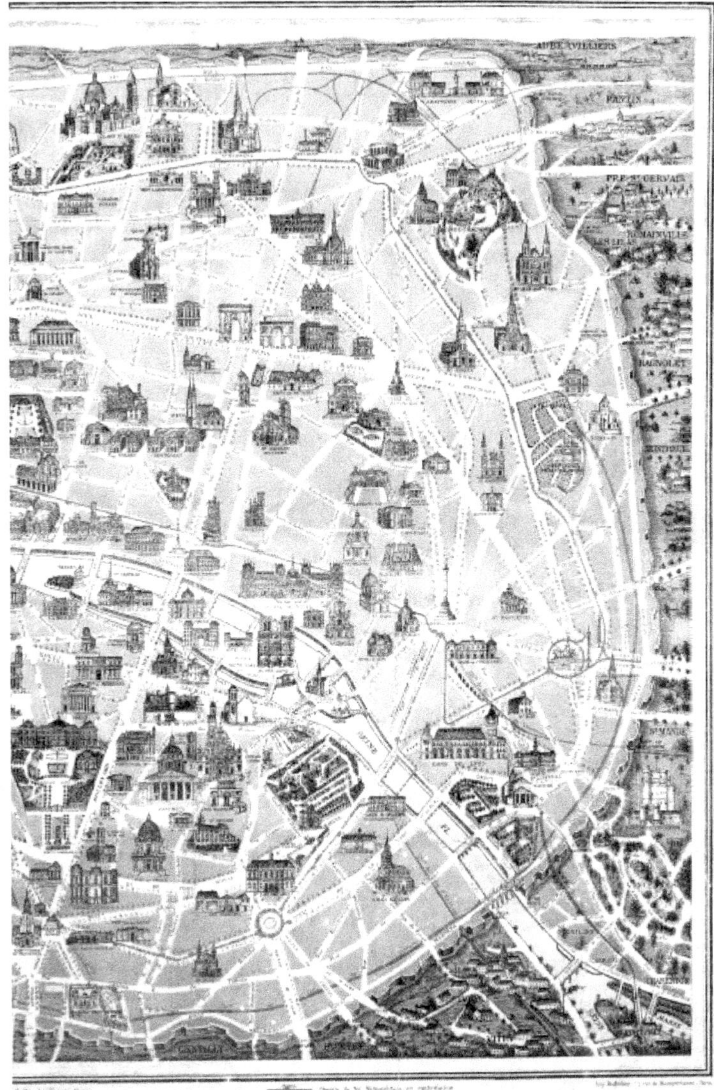

CHAPTER 1

Napoléon's Hand

Honora's troubles started years ago. The exact date was July 5, 2014, at precisely 2:10 p.m. How could she ever forget it? She was blindsided.

The fifth of July was the national day of reckoning for all high school graduates in France. Test results were released for the French national baccalaureate examination—most people called it "le Bac." Honora Favre sat for the very long, arduous, gut-wrenching exam the month before, along with hundreds of thousands of other young French graduates around the world. More than 80 percent of those taking le Bac passed. Honora was not particularly worried and assumed that she would perform well on the exam. Then life happened. She did not pass—not even close.

Failing le Bac once was terrible enough. But when Honora failed the exam a second time in June 2015, the private and public humiliation came crashing down on her pretty, soft, white shoulders. Instantly and permanently, it made Honora a second-class citizen socially and academically.

The expensive, strict, daily tutors that had drilled Honora to prepare for the second Bac gave favorable reports to Jacques and Chantal Favre, Honora's concerned parents. The tutors were sure that the Favres' daughter knew the exam material, and there was every reason to expect that she would pass on the second try—her last chance to take le Bac.

"Pas de problème, pas de souci." All three tutors—literacy, mathematics, and sciences—assured everyone that there would be "no problem, no worries" with Honora's success the next time.

Despite all her preparations, Honora froze from head to toe when she took her seat at the second Bac that fateful June 5, 2015. Walking into the huge examination hall that morning and taking her assigned seat, she didn't feel particularly afraid or nervous. She simply went catatonic when the proctor handed her the exam booklets; the months of knowledge drilled into her young, pretty head congealed like slush. She could not even sense that three and a half hours had passed while she just sat in her seat without even reading the questions. It was all over by lunchtime. She didn't bother to return for the afternoon session.

Honora's beloved Maman et Papa were *avocats à la Cour*, litigation lawyers. They were busy, exacting, disciplined, positive-thinking people who never imagined that anyone of their flesh, blood, and bone could fail—not at anything as important as le Bac. After the second fail, Honora could feel a sharp, acidic, uncomfortable change in how her parents treated her, looked at her, and talked about her to others. She was their only child. They failed as parents, they thought.

Never before had Honora felt so wounded, like she was kicked in the gut. The embarrassing news about her second flunk spread fast in her circle of friends and their parents. Almost overnight, she became a pariah.

I've got to buck up and get over this. It's not like I am dead, pregnant, or hooked on crack or some other disgraceful shit. It's just a test. There is a lot of other stuff out there that I will be able to do. Going to university is not everything. I'll show 'em. She always thought more clearly while soaking in her oval, white marble bathtub. She was waiting for the hair conditioner to work. A big mop of wet hair was twisted on top of her head. Honora's cerebrum was ticking very well indeed while she soaped her long, smooth, bronze legs and inspected the pink polish on her toes for chipping.

She was part of a small, intellectual clique of girls and boys who took more or less the same senior classes. These were her best *amis* at the private Lycée Albert de Mun, and each one of her friends passed le Bac. Except Honora. Many in her circle passed with mention très bien—very high honors. Honora didn't flinch when they told her. She instantly flashed a smile of congratulations, well-rehearsed in advance. At least while her friends were around, Honora tried hard to mask the shame and envy she could feel blistering inside her.

The group met one final time in the quadrangle of the lycée after the test results were released. It was a casual goodbye reunion. Once she was alone outside the *lycée* and everyone went their separate ways, Honora regained her composure. *Thank God, they left.* Honora tried to stop the stinging thoughts darting through her head. But she couldn't. *All this stinking class—100 percent—passed, and some of them with very high honors! What in the hell is wrong with me? I'll feel better when I get home.*

She kicked off her brown, lace-up school shoes and collapsed on her canopy bed's fluffy, silk, peach-colored duvet. Her bedroom windows looked out on the front street—the rue de Constantine, 7th Arrondissement. Home to Honora was her parents' palatial apartment—part of a six-story, residential, Haussman-style period building constructed with natural stone, slate and wood.

The apartments in this rarefied edifice were not common "apartments" that ordinary people live in, but rather cavernous, light-filled residences adorned with handcrafted marble and parquet floors, crystal chandeliers, fancy fireplace mantels, and floor-to-ceiling windows that opened wide to some of the most spectacular views in Paris. Like most Haussman period buildings, this one had a huge, curved, marble- and-brass staircase next to the small elevator that accessed all residences.

The residences shared a common entry of tall, solid, oak double doors opening into a cobblestone courtyard originally designed for the fancy, horse-drawn carriages that transported the Paris bourgeoisie of la Belle Époque throughout the city. Only the Paris elite lived there, along with a few rich foreigners who only used their apartment for short visits.

Jacques and Chantal Favre were not locking for an extravagant residence so early in their marriage, but the opportunity literally walked into their office one day. When Honora was barely three years old and her parents were struggling to build their law firm or cabinet, a new client walked through their office doors. Wasif Mansour was an Egyptian billionaire. He hired them to liquidate a sizable property. Quickly. He had inherited it and didn't want another place in Paris. Price negotiable. "Yes, of course, Monsieur Mansour. Leave everything with us. Our cabinet has the full resources to put the property on the market with the best agents, negotiate terms favorable to you, and execute the sale—all without undue delay." Jacques Favre gave his assurances to the client as he saw him to the door. The couple gasped as they read the client's dossier together and saw the address—no. 11 rue de Constantine. It was next to the Hôtel des Invalides, commonly known as Napoléon's Tomb. Apartments like this one were like rare, priceless jewels; they almost never went on the market. With about three thousand square feet of interior space plus wide balconies off each principal room, it boasted a breathtaking view of the Esplanade des Invalides across the street.

The apartment was situated in a place of awe and wonder. The Esplanade was a sumptuous park in front of Napoléon's Tomb—a collection of museums and monuments glorifying the military history of France. It encompassed nearly one and a half million square feet of emerald-green turf filled with dozens of finely trimmed and shaped evergreen hedges and trees stretching from Napoléon's Tomb all the way to the

Tsar Alexander III Bridge at the Seine River. To honor the Russian Tsar for his alliance of peace with France in the late 1880s, the French government built the most extravagant and ornate bridge in Paris—with statuary literally covered in brilliant gold leaf at its four corners. A structure so picturesque that professional haute couture video and photo shoots were often observed by pedestrians crossing the imperial bridge.

Jacques and Chantal did not hesitate to make a decision. Within a few short weeks, the transfer documents were signed, and at the Banque Société Générale, Monsieur Maffei approved a sufficient amount of funding from the Favre Trust for the young family to purchase the apartment.

This was the only home Honora had ever known, and this was where she returned, feeling every bit a failure, after leaving her triumphant friends. It was her sanctuary. She was in a funk, reclining on a stack of goose down pillows on her canopy-covered bed. She loosened her ponytail of thick, wavy, chestnut-colored hair and shut her cat-like, green eyes, trying to make the outside world disappear. The rays of sunlight streaming through her windows highlighted the gold in her eyebrows and on the tips of her lashes. Her breathing was slow and deep.

Her face resembled a predatory animal in peaceful repose, ready to pounce on its prey at any moment. Paris was Honora's entire world for as long as she could remember. She existed in a cozy, gilded cocoon where everything was perfect and predictable. Until now.

Honora was oblivious to the fact that she had been competing for most of her short life in a tightly regulated, strict private school system. There were no students at Lycée Albert de Mun who were not from the upper classes of French society. Those classes were comprised of bankers, chiefs of industry, lawyers, doctors, and large landowners who emerged in a new stratosphere after the French Revolution of 1789. Socially, such people ranked below French royalty and nobility. However, they controlled the wealth and power of France from the early 1800s, known as la Période Napoléonienne. It was the same socio- economic class of people that governed France that fateful, miserable day when Honora found out she flunked le Bac . . . for the second time.

Nobody outside of the elite groups of society ever passed through the heavy oak portals of the lycée facing the protected and guarded rue d'Olivet, 7th Arrondissement. This was a sacrosanct area nestled in the exclusive Rive Gauche of Paris. It was flanked by Napoleon's Tomb and the ancient private gardens of Queen Marie de Medici, known as les Jardins du Luxembourg. Young Honora Favre was of this world by virtue of her birth and upbringing.

Like Jacques and Chantal Favre, their parents, and their grandparents before them, the French knew all about their rigid educational machine and accepted its inevitable consequences—good or bad. In 1804, a minor, uppity noble from a barren, remote little island known as Corsica pushed, prodded, and schemed to crown himself emperor of France at age thirty-five.

His name was Napoléon Bonaparte. The Corsican, as the old French establishment called him, immediately launched into a barrage of wars, edicts, and grand construction projects that would transform his adopted country. Forever.

For starters, Napoléon was adamant that his Great French Empire must produce educated, skilled, disciplined, and sophisticated young minds. His dream was to create a new class of young people from within the working classes of the French population. Their life purpose would be to conquer and own all of Europe and the Middle East, the French global empire that Napoléon was determined to forge. To do this, he decided to create a modern, aggressive, and scientific system of education that would be compulsory for all French children from ages three to eighteen.

The new education apparatus created a do-or-die comprehensive oral and written examination, mandatory for all French graduating students. It made no allowance for failure. Students failing the new examination, twice, were cut out of the educational system of advancement nationwide. Cut out for life. His new subjects and the Parisian newspapers were aghast when Bonaparte decided to even include girls in his scandalous experiment. Formal education had been almost exclusively for boys before Napoléon's new-fangled plan.

The emperor knew how to marshal his assets. Voilà. For the first time in its history, France came to have a homegrown, educated, and productive middle class.

More than two hundred years later, as Honora reposed on her bed, gazing up at the big hand-knotted rose motif in the center of the silk canopy, Napoléon's hand continued to steer the direction of France and its people. Bonaparte's system had made her a lifetime failure at the tender age of eighteen and hit her a second time at nineteen years old. To add insult to injury, Napoléon's casket lay just across the street from Honora's home—in a place of honor inside the Hôtel des Invalides.

True enough, Honora flunked le Bac—twice—and most likely could never present herself at the famous Sorbonne or any prestigious university. Recently, the Bac system had been reformed to provide the two-time failures with different ways to university. But such alternatives were not for people like Honora Favre. The truth was that she was branded an academic loser in her own country. But Honora knew that it was possible to change her future . . . if she acted quickly.

Maître Jacques Antoine Favre was the typical French paterfamilias. He was of average height among *les hommes français*—five feet, ten inches—yet he was more imposing than taller men. Honora's father possessed (and expressed) strong and definite opinions, not only pertaining to his business or family but to France in general. And he was usually right. His broad shoulders held up a large, square head of straight, black hair parted on the left side, dark-blue eyes, and the aquiline, pointed nose of his Celt ancestors.

Honora rarely saw her father in anything but his dark-blue or gray light-weight wool suits worn with a starched, white, wing-collar shirt, finished with a bordeaux or gold Hermès cravat. He liked looking the part of a top Parisian *avocat* for the simple reason that he was one. His regular, fifteen-hour-long days and nights of law practice had not allowed him to expand his girth like his old schoolmates. He was relentless with his diet. To Jacques Favre, meals were a necessary distraction and social gesture. No more.

It didn't take Honora long before she built up enough courage to ask her father for a job. *Le petit déjeuner* was a hurried affair at chez Favre. It lasted precisely twenty minutes, from 8 to 8:20 a.m., in which time her parents hurriedly ate a café au lait with a small brioche spread with orange marmalade. It was mid-July 2015, and Honora decided to wait until the middle of the week, Wednesday, to take her shot. Mondays, Honora recalled, were stressful mornings for Papa.

After taking her usual chair at the table, Honora watched her father closely until he was about halfway finished with his café. "If you will allow me, I want to work in your office, Papa. I am tired of feeling like a failure." There. She said it. It was a relief to get it out, and Honora exhaled. When he looked up at her with his dark, raised eyebrows, almost frowning, Honora quickly added, "Maybe you think that I am too young and silly, but I promise to apply myself wherever I am placed, learn my duties quickly, and work hard."

Papa looked down at his Figaro newspaper and methodically folded it in three parts, per his habit. After a few moments and a long, measured breath which was almost a sigh, he raised his head and looked inquisitively at his only child. His sapphire- blue eyes made a deliberate, piercing connection with her green eyes while Jacques Favre's razor-sharp mind crafted his answer. Then he finally spoke.

"I'll be proud—*fière*—to have you working as our office receptionist, my darling girl!" Papa's tone was warm and loving, although there was a hint of circumspection in his voice.

"But it's to be Maître or Monsieur le Maître when we are at my cabinet, Honora. I will not be Papa while we are there. The same for your mother. We are les patrons at the office. Understood, ma belle?"

During the exchange, Chantal Favre quietly entered the dining room and took her customary place at the right hand of her husband. That was her way. She never interrupted the head of the household while family business was being discussed. Honora's mother got on with her breakfast as usual. The only thing that Honora noticed was different with her was that before leaving for the office, she excused herself and headed back to her boudoir. The unexpected tears welling up in Chantal's eyes smudged her mascara.

And so began a career for Honora. The following Monday morning, Honora entered the breakfast dining room dressed in a navy-blue pencil skirt and a cream, silk blouse. Like proper French young ladies, she wore only translucent face powder and pink lipstick. Both were from the House of Guerlain, the only maquillage she knew how to buy. Her thick hair was pulled loosely into a chignon banane. To soften her French twist, she pulled out a small tuft of virgin hair in front of each ear and hand curled it. *Ça va.* Honora knew the finishing touch to her coiffure would work. She looked at the image in her dressing room's full-length mirror with a smile of satisfaction.

Bravo, très bien, chérie! Chantal Favre was impressed and pleased after inspecting her beautiful, grown gamine. Feeling pride for her girl, she took a small drink of her café au lait and a tiny bite of her brioche. Her emerald green, almond-shaped eyes focused on her sumptuous surroundings and her family. She witnessed a little part of her destiny unfold that morning.

C'est vrai? Chantal Louise Riaux Favre asked herself if it were really true. Was she this elegant, meticulous, forty-four-year-old wife, mother, daughter, and lawyer ensconced in her magnificent apartment overlooking the most beautiful city in the world? Lately, the odd gray strand had started to creep into her natural, reddish-blonde mane. But Chantal was still a size eight, five feet, six inches tall belle femme. She took comfort in that and vowed to do whatever it took to keep her lean, straight silhouette for a long time. No way. She would not follow those women avocats who had discreetly begun letting out their black court robes to conceal the creeping obesity. That was not an option for la Mâitre Favre, as the busy clerks at the Tribunals liked to call her.

CHAPTER 2

Pleasing Important People

The Favre law firm had always been situated on the Avenue d'Iéna off the Arc de Triomphe or the Étoile, as Parisians called it. In the early 1990s, Jacques and Chantal had met, studied together, and fallen in love at the Sorbonne School of Law. On their romantic Sunday afternoon strolls along the Champs d'Élysées, they dreamed about how they would build their law business as well as their family.

When an *À Vendre* sign suddenly appeared shortly after their graduation at a small, dilapidated hôtel particulier at no. 15 avenue d'Iéna, Jacques knew it would be perfect for his future cabinet. With his parents' blessing, the following week he put on his only "lawyer's suit" and marched into the old Banque Société Générale behind the place de l'Opéra. Jacques's appointment was precisely at 10 a.m., and Monsieur Maffei, the senior director responsible for the Favre

Trust, greeted him with a quick nod. "Follow me into my bureau, Jacques," he said in a courtly tone.

Precisely ninety minutes later, Jacques Antoine Favre, newly graduated avocat à la Cour Paris, walked out of the bank's fifteen-foot-high, glass- and-iron double doors with fifty-thousand euros deposited in his new business checking account. At twenty-five years old, he had taken the first portion of his deceased grandmother's largesse.

She would be proud and happy, Jacques mused as he walked past the place de l'Opéra and onto the rue de Rivoli, swarming with tourists. He was going to meet Chantal for a celebration coffee at the Café de Louvre inside the magnificent Pyramide du Louvre. It was an exciting, hectic time for the young lovers; their civil and religious wedding ceremonies were held the following week.

It did not take Jacques long to find the absentee owner of the stately old house, buy it with the trust fund down payment and a hefty mortgage, and transform it into the place of legal business for the exuberant, ambitious couple. They never looked back.

A baby girl made her début at the Clinique Sainte Thérèse Paris in spring 1996—just as the final touches were being made to the dramatic transformation of the Belle Époque structure that was to be the Favre cabinet. The new parents were thrilled and excited to begin their family and their law business at the same time. But neither slowed down the frenetic pace of their work. They were growing a stable of well-paying clientele at a steady, fast pace now; lucrative new cases seemed to walk in the door every week. There was way too much work to do.

Decades later, Mademoiselle Honora Blanche Favre, nineteen years old, would ring the doorbell at no. 15 avenue d'Iéna. She was coming to work for Papa. In France, it was understood and accepted that Maître Jacques Favre was *le patron*, or the boss, of the Favre law firm. Yes, his wife was also a fully licensed, practicing partner of the firm. The other lawyers and staff always addressed her as Maître, of course. But she was only the wife, or *la femme*, not le patron.

Honora walked in, beaming with anticipation at her new and very first job. Right off the bat, she saw that the staff was already aware of her new position.

"Bonjour Madame Paul, je suis prête." Honora was proud to report "ready" on her first day of work. She stood facing a five-foot, eight-inches tall, angular, fifty-five-year-old, white-haired woman. She was her parents' longest-serving employee. Christine Paul knew it all. She had been with them from the get-go. She was the administrative director of the firm, and her face showed it. She had deep furrows across her forehead, and her skin reminded Honora of the camel-hued leather seats of Papa's sparkling, new Peugeot 5008.

Le Cabinet Favre was Madame Paul's whole life, or so it seemed to her office minions. No one knew exactly what Paul did after hours. She worked 8:30 a.m. to 9 p.m., Monday through Friday, although she did observe the de rigueur two-hour lunch break taken by everyone else. Vacations were two weeks at Christmas and New Year and the first three weeks of

August when Paris shut down for the summer break. The Favres cherished Christine Paul, and they never intruded on her private life. Although not an avocat, she was the bulwark of their law business.

Of course, Honora knew about Madame Paul. What jolted her that first day of work was how much discretionary power she wielded inside the law firm—power over all the staff, including Honora, and over the everyday business operations of the cabinet, including the purchase of supplies and other daily expenditures. And Paul, surprisingly, also had clout and influence over the other lawyers who needed her on accounting, billing, and other things indispensable to manage their client files.

"*Très bienvenue*, Honora." Paul crisply uttered the typical welcome greeting as she quickly glanced at her old wristwatch. Yes, Madame still wore a wristwatch, a faded, metal wristband à la mode Michel Herbellin, and it said something about her. That glance jolted Honora's recollection of her new boss—of her obsession with punctuality. Growing up listening to her parents talk shop during their time *en famille*, Honora had heard weird stories about la Paul, as some employees called her in private. The most ominous was that la Paul had slivers of eyes in the back of her head, concealed by her white hair. It was said that Paul saw and heard everything that went on in the cabinet during work hours.

As a little girl, Honora could not understand if these silly stories about the notorious Madame Paul were jokes, insults, or the truth. Even now, on her first day of work, it still scared her a little that her new supervisor could be so vigilant. Could Madame Paul really be this menacing? It was this thought that Honora couldn't keep out of her head.

Her new life was not going as she expected. Not exactly, that is, but Honora tried to go with the flow. Papa did not take her to work as she had hoped. He often had to rush in a taxi to the Cour de Paris for an early court hearing. Neither did her mother, who rushed out of the apartment to meet her deadlines and attend to her hearings before the Tribunals. So, on most workdays, Honora took the Métro from her home station Invalides to the Champs-Élysées- Clemenceau stop. Never mind that it was a thirty- minute walk from there to avenue Iéna. It was exciting to walk along the famous shopping street to see what was new in the magnificent windows of Louis Vuitton and Cartier. On more hectic days or in bad weather, Honora had to change trains twice, at Le Tour Eiffel and then at Trocadero, to get to the Iéna Métro stop, which was much closer to no. 15.

Lunch breaks at the office were lonely too. Staff and lawyers had their plans or habits for spending the two-hour respite. So, Honora was mostly on her own during lunch breaks. She liked to window-shop along the many streets feeding into the vast Étoile circle, picking up a packaged sandwich and small Perrier water around the corner at Monop' along the way.

Some Friday lunches, her closest friend from lycée, Sandrine de Rochefort, would meet her around the corner at La Crèmerie restaurant. Sandrine never had trouble passing exams and had sailed through le Bac. She was studying music composition at the Sorbonne School of Music. The two young, beautiful femmes delighted in sharing a *salade niçoise* and later a café noir over occasional Friday lunches. Honora was happy for her dear friend and the progress she was making at the venerable music conservatory where the greatest musical minds of France had studied.

At their last Friday lunch, Honora had learned of Sandrine's new love interest and suitor. "*Voici moi et Richard. Il est beau, hein?*" Sandrine showed Honora her phone with an image of her and Richard Lambert embraced casually in the school quadrangle. The gorgeous blond-haired, blue-eyed guy towered over her petite, brunette friend in the photo, but they looked happy together. Actually, more than happy. They looked like two people in love with a strong, physical attraction to each other.

Honora didn't dare ask about the sex, but Sandrine must have sensed her friend's curiosity and volunteered some titillating bits. Yes, she engaged in *l'amour* with Richard but had been on the pill for months before their first time. He was incredible in bed. Too hot. She couldn't keep her hands off him when they were alone in his apartment, in a taxi, or even in an elevator. This was Sandrine's first carnal, lustful experience. Honora bit her lip while taking all this in. She didn't want to ask her friend if Richard felt the same way, but of course, she hoped Richard reciprocated in his passion for Sandrine and was not just enjoying a fresh, fast fuck.

I am not actually jealous, only concerned that Sandrine doesn't get hurt, Honora assuaged her self-doubts when thinking about the lovers. Long ago, Maman had told her how easily petty, negative feelings could contaminate Honora's heart if she wasn't careful.

In the beginning, staying clear of la Paul wasn't too tough. Honora kept Madame Paul at bay. Although only a beginner at handling receptionist work, she had mastered the delicate practice of how to greet and manage distinguished, anxious clientele on their arrival at the law firm. Taking them coffee when the coffee girl was too busy or didn't show up for work was not a problem for Honora. She liked pleasing important people.

As at most other prestigious cabinets d'avocats in Paris, arriving visitors were buzzed in after the receptionist inspected them on the security camera outside. Honora loved playing the part of the law firm's receptionist.

The reception hall was a pivotal post, so to speak, in the overall operations of the law firm. It was located inside the entry foyer of the renovated hôtel particulier. Although, at the time of the renovations, it was considered strange and disrespectful, Jacques Favre had instructed his architect to apply for, and aggressively pursue, obtaining a building permit from the city of Paris to demolish the dark, small entry hall of the old structure and replace it with a fifteen-foot-high, modern, glass-enclosed atrium. Thanks to family connections at l'Hôtel de Ville, the stately city hall of Paris, the permit was issued.

That grand entry—brilliant with the sun streaming through the glass ceiling—was Honora's responsibility. She sat proudly behind the three and a half-foot-high, ten-foot-wide, curved stone counter, mostly checking appointments on the computer screen. Although not expected of her, Honora habitually rose to her feet and greeted law firm visitors warmly and respectfully. Many had come to know her already, and her welcome seemed to please them.

The scheduled deliveries of office supplies also were her responsibility, and she kept a close eye on each one, meticulously recording it in the spreadsheet on her computer.

Although Honora had to record all such deliveries, Christine Paul kept control of all delivery dates and what items would be delivered. Paul was the only one that communicated with the delivery man—Khaled. And the deliveries were always in the early morning before the typical arrival time for the avocats and the cabinet's clients. Nobody at the firm had the time or inclination to question la Paul or her management practices. They were either afraid or too busy producing the chargeable hours needed to keep the firm profitable. Jacques and Chantal Favre had complete trust in Madame Paul's administration of their cabinet. It was a blind trust.

Honora loved working at the law firm. She felt everything there was unique and special, particularly her receptionist's desk. Wanting to make a bold statement to arrivals at the firm, le patron ordered a solid, hand-chiseled, marble counter or reception desk from Carrara, Italy, soon after closing on his building. During weeks of wrangling via email with the famous Tuscan quarry, he insisted on buying only the rare, dove-gray-colored marble with subtle cream veining throughout. It was an extravagance that Jacques Favre rarely indulged in—but he was sure that it would pay off.

Mademoiselle Favre had started receiving her first-ever, bi-weekly paychecks. When she held the first one in her hand and read the amount next to her full, formal name, it was a thrill. *C'est vrai? Pour moi?* She was excited to get her first payment; she was a working woman now. Even as a lowly office receptionist, she was earning a real wage. Never mind that she received less than one-half of her earnings after paying income taxes, national health insurance, and the Métro travel card. Honora had enough to buy some nice, new things to wear, update her maquillage at Sephora, and get her coiffure at her usual Salon Alexandre on the rue de la Paix. Shopping gave Honora a high. Nothing was more exciting.

Everyone at the firm had always known that la Paul was a cold-blooded tyrant. The fear or dread of the beastly woman was something all the office staff shared and even some of the lawyers. It created a strange type of bond among most of the law firm employees, and so Honora began to feel she was part of the group. She was not alone, and she was no longer a pariah.

Since her first day at work in the summer of 2015, many big events had begun to reshape French daily routine. The Favre family was relieved that an ex-Rothschild wheeler-dealer and relative newcomer to France politics won the May 2017 presidential election. After a bitter campaign where radicals from the Left and the Right attacked him, Emmanuel Macron seemed to be a good choice to tackle the country's colossal economic and social problems. Even Honora voted for Macron, though she secretly favored the female candidate, Marine Le Pen.

On her daily commutes on the Métro or just walking along the Seine, Honora had started to get wolf whistles and looks from young men of various sorts. Construction workers along the road, young, professional travelers standing next to her on the Métro, riding in the same elevator, at the stops—in the most unexpected places, Honora began to experience the opposite sex reacting to her young, vibrant, feminine mystique.

She was slim-hipped and somewhat tall, and her long legs were lean, lightly bronzed, and youthful. She was now twenty-one years old, and since becoming a working woman, her beauty had evolved from cute schoolgirl to feminine chic and provocatively Parisian. For the first time in her life, Honora knew the sensation of being attractive to men and the strange raw power that comes with that.

The adolescent boys at her collège and later at the Lycée Albert de Mun never made any lasting impression on her. But she was a belle femme now, complete with bubbling hormones. Sometimes Honora thought about Sandrine's intense entanglement with her lover, Richard, although she did not want to get into anything that complicated. At least for now.

La fête de Noël 2018 was a joyful time for Jacques and Chantal Favre. Over the past two years, they transformed their small cabinet into a litigation juggernaut— launching incessant motions, objections, requests, and challenges to the tribunal judges. They had gone into the lion's den of the highest appellate court in France to fight the toughest lawsuit of their careers. And they had won. The contingency fee agreed years earlier with their client, a large Algerian trading concern, came out to two and a half million euros after deducting out-of-pocket expenses. Not bad for working an average of twelve hours a day for the past two years. The windfall was shared with all the lawyers, even the junior clerks.

Everybody went home that December 21 feeling jubilant and special after the sumptuous Christmas lunch—fête de Noël—which the law firm had hosted in the grande salon of the stunning hotel Le Bristol Paris. Attending a party on the venerable rue du Faubourg Saint-Honoré across the street from the official presidential residence—Palais de l'Élysée— was not a regular activity for most of the law firm's employees. It was a generous, special gesture of appreciation from their bosses—les Maîtres Favre. The employees looked forward to it every Christmas.

"Bonjour! Ça va?" The lawyers and staff happily greeted each other as each one came into the office that first workday of the New Year 2019, the second week of January. They were relaxed and refreshed

from the long traditional break and were anxious to return to their daily deadlines and schedules of hurried client meetings, rushed writing of pleadings, and then jumping in taxis, smock and wig in hand, to argue in front of the Paris judges.

The whole firm was excited to be back in the office, and there was fresh gossip that a new lawsuit was in the works. Bigger and better paying than even the Algerian one. Perhaps not wanting to spoil the excitement over the new client, there was no office talk about the notorious *Gilets jaunes*—yellow vests.

These working-class men and women, young and old, organized swiftly at the close of 2018 into a national Yellow Vest Movement of angry, frustrated, and desperate citizens who saw their government taking more and more of their shrinking paychecks every year. The movement seemed to be spreading everywhere. It used social media to attract hundreds of thousands of protesters each weekend.

What jump-started the yellow vests was President Macron's new tax on fuel consumption. Although the new tax would be only pennies per gallon, the average working French citizen was already drowning in taxes and government fees, charges, and horrific import duties on daily necessities. Together, the national, departmental, and municipal taxing authorities were already taking nearly 70 percent of a worker's income.

Older French citizens remembered when their daily baguette cost one franc—the old currency before the European Union bureaucrats took over. Now it cost seven times that—one euro. The yellow vests were citizens disgusted with their worsening quality of life and the big holes in their pockets from taxes on everything.

President Macron thought he had concocted a novel way to increase revenues for his shrinking treasury—tax gasoline and heating fuel because it helped climate control. Clever rationalization, he thought. He was desperate to feed the hungry beast of the National Welfare System. By most accounting standards, the system had become insolvent long ago and currently operated in the red with a fast-growing deficit. Put simply, the treasury of France was broke.

In early 2019, the yellow vests were not backing down despite a massive police presence at each protest. With each passing week, their grassroots leadership shot back with more demands to Macron's vulnerable government. The authorities were on the defensive, and the public outcry against tough police tactics to subdue the riots was increasing daily. It was a kind of civil war, although nobody dared to call it that. Despite all of this, nobody at the Favre law firm appeared especially worried.

"These yellow vest troublemakers need to go out and get a job," Jacques Favre explained to his family over dinner one cold January night. "It's just a mob. *Bientôt, les bètes sauvages se lasseront et abondonneront.*" Favre expected the savages would soon tire and be finished with their nonsense. He was sure of it. Like many of his class, he saw the protesters as lazy, worthless vagrants rather than everyday, working people enraged at their country's unquenchable, oppressive fiscal regime.

Honora was excited to return to work following the long Christmas break. She missed her responsibilities over the reception hall and over cabinet deliveries. When she asked Madame Paul about reconciling the entries on her spreadsheet with what was actually in the supply room, she was told to mind her own business. According to Honora's meticulous records, it appeared that roughly half of the sealed boxes had disappeared while the office was closed over the holidays. La Paul didn't seem concerned when Honora mentioned the discrepancy a second time.

CHAPTER 3

Follow the Music

It was hard to believe that it was 2019, and Mademoiselle Favre had been at her job three and a half years. Strangely, after years of positive evaluations and small merit raises for her services, Honora still couldn't shake the fear and trepidation of her boss, Madame Paul.

Honora never forgot that she could never be late to work—not ever. The fear of being late had morphed into a weird phobia for Honora. It was the *bête noir* of her boss, Christine Paul. Even when not at work, she found herself compulsively looking at her phone to check the time. She had nightmares of being fired by la Paul for being late. Some of her colleagues had, in fact, been fired for being only a few minutes late, although Honora never thought it could happen to her. It was her parent's cabinet after all. La Paul, a mere employee, wouldn't dare fire the bosses' daughter.

Would she?

But the yellow jackets were getting worse now, blocking more streets and shutting down more Métro lines with every passing week. Getting from one place to another in central Paris was becoming extremely precarious.

On weekdays, Honora was out the door well ahead of first light. Because of Madame Paul, Honora had a fraught routine of rising by 4 a.m. to jump in a hot shower, do her coiffure and maquillage for the day, and slip into her work ensemble, carefully chosen and laid out the night before. Before going to bed, it had become her private ritual to think about and then carefully lay out her dress or skirt, blouse, and blazer with coordinating Hermès Carré or Gavroche scarf, shoes, and simple pearl or gold ear studs. She loved her dressing alcove with the full-length, beveled mirror framed in antique silver just outside her walk-in closet. It was her favorite part of the huge family apartment. Getting herself ready for work in the dark, early morning hours was like donning her armor. With her armor, Honora felt beautiful, prepared, and empowered for the workday ahead.

Like Papa, breakfast was an afterthought for Honora. If she was up before her parents, she raced into the kitchen alone to make a tall Nespresso and warm a madeleine cake in the microwave. Breakfast was consumed in minutes, standing at the kitchen island.

The year was flying by. That was the first flash in Honora's mind as she looked at the tiniest first buds on the London Plane sycamore trees lining the Champs d'Élysée. A sure sign that spring was coming. She had just picked up some Guerlain lip liner with matching gloss at la grande boutique Sephora on that street. She didn't dwell too long on the realization that Papa was wrong about the *Gilets jaunes*. They had not tired and gone away. Au contraire. Facing escalating riots, police were now beating and throwing smoke bombs at women, children, and even handicapped yellow jackets in wheelchairs. This was happening all over central Paris and other large cities, like Toulouse and Lyon. She had never lived through anything like it and had started to worry that she would become trapped in the throngs of rioters and get beaten to the ground by the mob or the police.

Recently, Madame Paul gathered all the staff in the large conference room. "Everyone in this room is expected to do whatever they need to do to arrive here no later than 8:30 a.m. No matter what happens from here on with the *Gilets jaunes*. Understood?"

Her low, guttural tone was the one she used for commands or threats. No one in the group said anything, but faint murmurs or moans were heard. Sad and embarrassed for her coworkers, Honora just looked out the window, away from la Paul. She knew that some staff had to travel more than two hours—each way—from suburbs like Mantes-la-Jolie even before the yellow vests' shutdowns. "You are dismissed, if there are no questions." Paul then motioned with her eyes for everyone to exit the room through the tall, glass, double doors of the conference room.

Spring in Paris was typically a glorious time when gardens everywhere entered full bloom. But this year, people didn't have the luxury of noticing anything but the worsening riots. Public transportation, which nearly everyone depended on, was shut down en masse. In their frenzy of rage and violence, the yellow vests did not think about or care that the people being significantly hurt, physically and economically, were their very own—men and women who had to get to work every day to earn a living.

It was still pitch-black outside when Honora reached the Invalides Métro stop in the predawn hours of Thursday. She nearly lost her balance running down the concrete stairs descending to the train platforms. She saw that the metal grill doors to the underground entrance were shut—locked with a huge padlock. A dirty piece of torn cardboard had been hung from the padlock. Some stressed out Métro employee, oblivious to grammar and spelling, had hastily thrown up a makeshift sign announcing *Fermtoor xseptionel jusqu'à 15 mai*.

"*MERDE!*" Honora blurted out loud in the darkness. It was shit to her—rushing to the Métro to find this.

No Métro for the next two damned weeks! Tiny daggers jabbed quickly, sharply inside her head. How could she be left without Métro transport across the Seine to get to the cabinet? The next station was at least an hour walk away, and she didn't even know if that was open.

Those were her last thoughts before Honora's mind went blank, standing at the locked metal doors of the Invalides Métro. Once she regained her composure,

Honora couldn't tell how long she had just stood there. She was in a stress-induced trance with panicked commuters rushing about and ignoring the attractive, chic young woman who didn't move a muscle. Her phone showed that it was 5:30 a.m.—the onslaught of the Paris rush hour.

She couldn't even jump into a taxi. The stands were empty. Her last resort—Uber—wouldn't even open to the app's home screen! So, Honora did the only thing she could think of: she steadily walked the more than two-mile jaunt to 15 avenue d'Iéna. It was 7:43 a.m. when Honora dragged herself into the office, dirty, tousled, and exhausted. Her hair and makeup were a sweaty mess. Her new Roger Vivier black patent leather flats were filthy and scuffed.

Bravo! I made it in record time. The young receptionist was relieved and pleased with herself. As Honora used her e-key to unlock the giant doors, she thought she saw Khaled's black delivery van speeding away from the front curb, tires screeching. *No. It couldn't be. He never delivers this early,* Honora thought to herself.

After Honora recovered in the toilette dames, she walked around the silent offices and hallway. Only Madame Paul was there, and she looked wasted. Honora had never seen la Paul with wrinkled clothes and smeared makeup. Before she could control her expression, a smirk shot out from Honora. Madame looked like an aging clown! Honora snapped back into office mode and did a crisp, respectful, "Bonjour, Madame." Heading to the safety of the coffee room, she realized that the old tyrant had not left the office from the day before. Where exactly did Paul sleep? Did she sleep? Was it cruel to smirk at a tired, old woman?

Christine Paul had been ignoring insults and ridicule from those around her for a long time—as long as she could remember. "Pas grave," she told herself. In the grand scheme of things, Honora was no more than a pesky gnat to la Paul. Most important, the gnat had not seen what Paul had received and quickly smuggled into the supply closet that morning. Her runner had made a clean getaway.

More and more often, Honora had been putting her head down in the coffee room during her afternoon breaks. She felt more drained and exhausted every day. Her office mates acted like they didn't notice.

"*Bon courage, ma Chérie*," quipped Jacques Favre the following morning as he darted out the apartment door. It was the first Friday in May, 4:45 a.m. Papa's voice woke Honora. He rarely left for work before she did. She glanced out the hall window overlooking the central cobblestone courtyard of their building. Omar, the long-time driver for the Favre family, was opening the door to the car, and the trunk was loaded with familiar luggage. Her parents were leaving to catch the first departure from Orly to London Heathrow.

Honora had forgotten that Maman had told her about the trip and that Honora would be on her own for that weekend until the following Wednesday. She didn't remember going back to bed after her parents left for the airport. She didn't remember falling back into a paralyzed sleep as her head fell on the pillow.

Mozart's "Allegro" from *A Little Night Music*

blasted from her iPhone. *Who could be calling so early in the morning? Is it Maman or Papa from the airport?* These thoughts flashed into Honora's sleepy, groggy brain. When she woke up enough to stretch to her bedside table to reach her phone, she shrieked, "Mon Dieu!"

The screen showed 10:45 a.m. and a missed incoming call from the firm's main number but no message recorded. Honora called the cabinet. She didn't recognize the voice that answered, but a pleasant-sounding, young woman put her through to Madame Paul.

"*C'est terminé, Honora! Ne prenez pas la peine de revenir.*" You are finished here, Honora. Don't bother to return.

Then la Paul hung up.

Stunned. Honora had just been fired from her parent's law firm by an old witch who didn't even give her a chance to explain! What is happening to me? Will I ever stop being a loser? These things churned viciously inside her head as Honora sat on the edge of her tousled, peach-colored sheets and duvet.

It was now nearly noon on Friday, and it had started to rain in Paris. Honora could smell the rain-soaked trees and flower boxes in the street from inside her bedroom. The aroma was delicious and soothing. Showers like this washed away the Parisian traffic fumes—at least temporarily.

Honora pulled on some black leggings, her Nikes, and a dirty T-shirt that read I Love New York. She needed to walk this out. So, Honora headed out the front door of her building, crossed the Esplanade, sprinted across the Tsar Alexander III bridge, and kept walking in long, quick strides along the right bank of the Seine. She didn't know exactly where her body was taking her or how far. And she didn't care. She just wanted to get away from her shock and disappointment—if that was even possible. Confusion set in as many thoughts ran through her head: Why did she fire me for being late one goddamn time? Is there another reason why she wanted me out of there? Honora couldn't understand why one screw-up justified such a harsh, permanent punishment.

Tears streamed down her face, and her breath was heavy with all the congestion in her head. Gradually, the chaos inside subsided, and her walking pace slowed. Her mind seemed to get back in control of the rest of her body. Her eyes focused on a familiar place. The bustling Place de Trocadero and Palais de Chaillot stood just ahead. Lunchtime was winding up in the many outside restaurants along the square, and diners were waving at the garçon to pay their addition and rush back to work.

She walked the whole way around the Trocadero square to stand on the immense viewing platform next to the Palais de Chaillot. Honora stood looking at the Eiffel Tower in all its glory. So were hundreds of foreign tourists, mostly Asian. They were excited to be there and were happily taking photos of the magnificent sight. A woman walked away from her tourist group toward Honora and used her primitive, touristy French to ask, *"Boo prendre photo, Madamzelle?"*

She was about the age of her mother and had a warm, friendly smile. Honora didn't mind her bad accent and accepted the phone from the woman's outstretched hand. Trying to clear her throat—raw from the wind and crying—she tried to muster the kindest, most normal voice possible under the circumstances. *"Mais oui, avec plaisir, Madame."* Honora responded that, of course, it would be her pleasure to do so.

In that instant, Honora shook off her anxiety or depression or whatever had been controlling her and realized something. She was dirty, crumpled, and probably disoriented—like a person living on the street. She also had no money, not even her phone. She had run out of the apartment with only a key. *Never mind,* she thought. *I must help these people get their photos taken here and then go.*

As Honora took the tourists' photo, she heard familiar music playing somewhere just ahead across the river. The music caressed Honora, and it pulled her toward something or someone. The voice in her head told her to follow the music. The young gendarme at the Pont d'Iéna smiled at Honora despite her being in shambles. With an admiring twinkle in his eyes, he told her, "You can cross the bridge, Mademoiselle; it is now open for pedestrians." Honora had walked down to the Seine to try to get across the river to the place from where the music seemed to be coming.

Finally, she saw it. The children's carousel played music from her favorite movie, Mary Poppins. Next, she heard "My Favorite Things" from The Sound of Music. It was mid-afternoon and still drizzling. Only a handful of toddlers—too young to be in school—were there with their nannies.

There was a beautiful black stallion with a red-and-gold saddle, bridle, and stirrups on the carousel. It beckoned her to ride. *Pourquoi pas?* she thought—why not? Only two infants were mounted and ready to ride on the carousel, and each was held steady by their vigilant nanny.

The carousel attendant had snuck around the back for a cigarette break when Honora jumped on the carousel, and it started to move. Then, "A Spoonful of Sugar" started to play. Perfect. Riding round and round felt like a huge release to Honora. No yellow jackets, no shutdown, and no la Paul. She began to feel the cool, crisp air blowing on her face as she rode the stallion. It was dry now; she had run out of tears. When the attendant returned, he didn't seem bothered that Honora never produced her ticket.

Once the carousel stopped and she dismounted, Honora visualized her new objectives. *Now I must figure out my plan of action*, reflected Honora.

CHAPTER 4

Omaha

For the past few weeks after Honora's termination from the cabinet, Jacques and Chantal had looked the other way. Yes. They were disappointed with Madame Paul's abrupt treatment of their daughter; but the smooth and profitable operation of their business was a priority. And Paul was irreplaceable, at least for the short term. It was July 2019—the busiest July ever at the Favre law firm. The hours at work were long, and Honora's parents didn't have the time or the energy to focus on their daughter's problems. So, they gave their daughter some breathing space and simply enjoyed her company at the dinner table without asking too many questions. Reassuring each other in their private moments, they agreed that their beloved girl was just passing through a rough time.

Honora would soon find another job or, even better, find a young, ambitious avocat to marry and start her own family. Naturally, Honora's big stumbles would be forgotten. She would get on with her life as it should be: Parisian, traditional, and secure. The Favres were about to swallow a painful dose of reality.

Now that Honora had made her big decision at the Tour d'Eiffel carousel, she was determined to produce a plan and act on it. It was going to be a D-Day, of sorts, for Honora Favre—that is how the anxiety felt in the back of her throat. She usually didn't back away from confrontations with her parents before this dilemma. But this was a different kettle of fish—it was going to be a battle to liberate herself from her Parisian life, her home in the grandiose apartment on the rue de Constantine, her friends, her surroundings, and everything that she depended on for her daily existence and for her identity.

Maman and Papa definitely will not like it. I love them dearly and don't want them to be hurt. But I will not surrender to what they want for me or go back to any other job here. These thoughts kept playing in Honora's mind—day and night—while trying to put together the details of her liberation from Paris.

Although she was born generations after it happened, Honora knew all about D-Day, commonly called le Débarquement. It was that momentous day when hundreds of thousands of soldiers, tanks, jeeps, trucks, and planes swept into her country along the beaches of La Manche to liberate France from Hitler's Nazi war machine. The monsters occupied, ransacked, and plundered France and other neighboring countries during nearly four and a half horrific years. Nearly everyone in France, including children, suffered greatly, and many died during the German occupation.

Grand-père Maurice told Honora all about D-Day—many times—during the annual summer vacations on the family farm. Her grandfather was a spunky thirteen-year-old farm boy on June 6, 1944, when D-Day or the Battle of Normandy began. The memories of that day and the ensuing weeks lived in his memory seventy-five years later as if they were recent occurrences. Maurice's face sparkled with excitement every time he spoke of those dangerous times.

The Riauxs of Normandy hunkered down on their farm during the terrors of the Nazi Occupation in France, which lasted from 1940 to 1944. After the American and English military stormed Omaha and Gold Beaches and expelled the Germans from Normandy, the clan bounced back quickly. Grand-père never stopped working, planting, and harvesting his fields—now with modern, expensive New Holland equipment—despite his advanced age and encroaching arthritis in his knees and back.

What drove him every day was the thought that he was wanted and needed by his only son and now his grandson, who had become the principal owners of the family agriculture business. Eighty-eight-year-old Maurice felt happy and prosperous as he joined them out in the fields six days a week. What never left him were the recollections—in vivid detail—of the hellish events of his youth and the glory of the D-Day liberation.

The idyllic, long, sunny days in the heart of ancient Normandy with Grand-père and Grand- mère Riaux grew a strong backbone in Honora. The lessons she learned from her maternal grandparents fortified her—even as a little girl. Audrey-Marie and Maurice Riaux loved la petite Honora and relished the three short weeks in August when they had her on their farm outside Bonneville-Aptot, a remote region inhabited by native Normand families who had always worked on the land. Direct blood descendants of the Norsemen or Viking tribes that had invaded and conquered northwestern France in the eighth century, the locals here identified themselves foremost as Normands and marginally as French. There were barely four hundred residents.

Bonneville had a charming, red-brick, two-story Mairie, or town hall, and a carved stone memorial to its residents who had fallen in World War I, but it had no commercial establishments of any kind. Although the village and surrounding fields and forests sat on an immense, flat, granite plateau, the soil there was dark, heavy, and rich with nutrients. Fields on the plateau had been cultivated for more than two thousand years.

This was evident from the primitive tools that a field hand sometimes would find while tilling the soil—smooth, shiny pieces of stone or fossilized wood, ancient objects made with the strong hands of prehistoric inhabitants for slaughtering wild animals or working the land.

Wheat, linen, sugar beets, and all manner of vegetables and fruit grew in abundance, and farmers sometimes could plant and harvest three rounds in a single year from their fields. Most Sundays, they would bathe and put on their best clothes to drive to the nearby capital of Normandy—Rouen—to attend Holy Mass. These simple yet devout people felt especially blessed when they worshipped inside the Church of St. Joan of Arc, constructed on the hallowed ground where St. Joan of Arc was burned alive multiple times in the year 1431 for the crime of heresy.

The old Riaux couple sometimes took little Honora to Holy Mass in Rouen and later proudly strolled with her along the cobblestone streets around le Vieux Marche. It was a lively farmer's market that existed since les vieux temps where the freshest local produce, meats, and fish were sold daily, even on Sundays. It was not known how long the market had existed but it was already a thriving concern when St. Joan was publicly executed a stone's throw away.

Tiny Honora was special to both of them, but particularly to Grand-père Riaux. He never forgot that their adorable granddaughter had taken her first steps along the long rows of *pommiers* on his lands. The rows of apple trees extended as far as the eye could see; it was a joy for Grand-père to feel the lively toddler's tiny, soft fingers inside his rough, steady hand as he guided her through the orchards. Honora never forgot the love and security she felt among the rows of apple trees and the stories told by her grandfather.

Although Grand-mère had passed years ago and Honora's parents no longer had time for the long August visits to Normandy, the history and fervor that captivated Honora those summer holidays were carved into her psyche. They were a permanent part of her.

Now twenty-three years old, Honora was preparing for her own Débarquement. Part one was beginning a dialogue with her parents about leaving home. The dialogue would be her Omaha Beach— the first tranche of a long, arduous battle. Her body tensed up just thinking about it.

The 2019 August holiday break was about to begin, and the Favre law firm was winding up pending hearings and discovery proceedings to shut down for the next three weeks. On the last day before the long-awaited break, Honora arranged an evening at home with her parents to launch her Omaha.

It was after eight in the evening, and the Favres were relieved to get home and relax in their grand salon lined with white-and-gold boiseries. The room was the pièce de résistance of the Favre home, and Chantal loved looking at the ornate, seventeenth-century wood panels she had rescued from an abandoned Rouenese mansion. Although the room was filled with antiques, Chantal's favorite furniture was the matching pair of canary- yellow, silk canapés stuffed with the softest goose down from Zurich. The long, sleek sofas faced each other in the center of the salon. Through a cherished client years ago, she was introduced to a silk weaver in Lyon who made the silk upholstery according to her vision—a subtle pattern of fleur-de-lis interspersed with their joint initials CFJ.

When her parents walked in, Honora was in the salon, standing next to the low, Chinese, black, lacquer-topped table in between the canapés. She was prepared and determined.

C'est fou! Impossible! Hors de question, ma petite! She growled like a lioness without actually raising her voice. Tough, cynical litigator Chantal Louise Riaux Favre reached down in her gut and pulled out her baritone voice to talk to her daughter. Maître Favre never spoke like this outside the courtroom. It was unfeminine and intimidating. She certainly never imagined using this tone with her precious girl. But she had to nip this insanity in the bud. What she was hearing from Honora about leaving Paris was crazy. It was impossible. Out of the question.

Chantal had been born and reared on the Riaux farm, although her education took her to Paris at an early age to enroll at the Lycée Albert le Mun. As it turned out, young Chantal became a Parisian and never returned to live in Normandy, although she kept in close contact with her beloved parents and her big brother, Eric. Hearing Honora's ridiculous proposals to move to Normandy, Chantal's Riaux blood boiled to the surface that evening in the salon. Her Normand blood. The blood of the savage, invincible Viking founders of Normandy. *What a spoiled ingrate! What did we do wrong to raise such an imbecile who now wants to run away to live like an ignorant peasant? What will she do in that poor, dirty place?* Honora's mother had never entertained such thoughts, such lowly opinions of her only offspring. Tragic!

She stood up from one of the yellow canapés, marched over to the mirrored bar in the corner of the room, and did something totally out of character. She reached for the bottle of Domaine Dupont Calvados kept on the highest glass shelf. This Normand delicacy brandy—aged thirty years in oak barrels— was served by the Favres only to distinguished guests or the most prestigious clients after a formal dinner. The bottle was rarely opened.

"Desperate measures for desperate times. I need to calm my nerves and get back in control of this situation. *Toute de suite!*" Chantal Favre murmured to herself as she emptied the bottle into a sparkling Baccarat tumbler, filling it to the top. Then, while still standing, she chugged it down. All of it. Honora said nothing. She had never seen her mother like this.

While Honora explained to her parents that she could no longer live in Paris and was leaving for Grand- père's farm to find a job in Normandy, Jacques Favre had kept his place in the big, blue velvet fauteuil in a corner of the salon. It was his customary seat, his throne of sorts, from which he liked to observe the goings on. He did not speak. His back remained reclined in the cushy, overstuffed chair. Jacques held back even during his wife's Calvados episode. Only the slight twitch on his left temple demonstrated his frame of mind. His neurons were in overdrive, engineering some response to his daughter's perilous plans.

Once the Calvados's sugar and alcohol kicked in, Chantal started to cry. Sob, actually. In between sobs, she looked across the room at Honora and asked, "How can you stab Papa and me in the heart like this, ma chérie? Do you hate us so much that you would run away to some backwater and dirty your hands with whatever menial job you can find? Jacques, please say something! Do something!"

A few seconds passed while Honora's father took a deep breath, still seated in the fauteuil, and then he stood up. Honora and Chantal gazed at his commanding posture and facial expression. He looked like a warrior going into battle in a trial before the highest court in the land, le Cour de Cassaton.

That is the impression that he gave to his wife and daughter at that tense moment. Jacques' body language was formidable, but as it turned out, his tone and words were warm, nurturing, and loving.

"Chérie, Honora, you are everything to your mother and me. Our whole world. I know you must think we are too busy to love you or care about your problems. But that is not true. Your happiness and security are extremely important to us. What will you do if you run away to Grand- père at the farm? He is too old to look after you or find you a job. Nothing out there is suitable for a proper Parisian girl like you."

Chantal walked over to Honora's side while listening to her husband's discourse. She gently draped her arm around Honora's stiffened shoulders. Her primal, maternal instincts told her that protecting her daughter was paramount. She would not let her roam aimlessly around Normandy and be a burden to her old grandfather.

Worst of all, Honora would be an embarrassment to the Riauxs of Normandy once the local families discovered that she failed le Bac twice and could never go to a university. No. Chantal could not allow it.

After Jacques finished speaking—only a matter of a few minutes—he felt satisfied with the words spoken to his darling girl. He believed that they would turn the tide of Honora's rebellion and that she would give up her silly plan and stay in Paris. He walked over to his wife and daughter and joined their embrace. *This is my family, and we will stay together. No matter what.* This thought was firmly fixed in Jacques Favre's heart and mind. He would not bend.

A couple of minutes after the family embrace, Honora relaxed and regained her composure, and so did her mother. Chantal could smell the scent of Calvados oozing from her pores. How could she succumb to such stupid theatrics in front of her belle gamine? "Please. Can we talk about this tomorrow? It's the beginning of our long vacation. Papa and I are exhausted from work. Let's sleep late and then have our *petit dejeuner en famille.* I promise you that we will find a solution. *Je t'aime ma petite.*"

"*Je t'aime aussi, Maman et Papa.*" Honora's voice softly quivered as she told her parents that she loved them too. But her resolve was intact. She was a Favre, after all, and like her father, she would not retreat from her decision.

The first-class car was nearly empty. When Honora purchased her train ticket on the SNCF website, she paid the extra fare for a reserved seat. She bought the ticket days before that final, unhappy confrontation with her parents. Of course, she did not tell her parents about the ticket. She had been a little disingenuous during their heated, emotional discussion the night before. I had to do it, and I am not sorry, she told herself. The one-way ticket to Bernay, Eure, Normandy, was her insurance policy that she would leave Paris. No matter what her parents said or did that last evening together in the salon. She took a forward-facing window seat two rows from the door in car number eight, Première Classe, departing from Paris Gare Saint Lazare, final destination Deauville/ Honfleur.

Her three Longchamp jumbo totes were bursting full. She hoped the zippers would hold. Her seat was not far from the luggage racks because she wanted to keep a close eye on her belongings. They held most of her worldly possessions, except for her sac à dos filled with her Vuitton wallet, MacBook Pro, phone, toiletries, and maquillage. The backpack never left her person. It was her survival kit.

Honora was wide awake when the train pulled out of the station precisely on schedule at 6:30 a.m. It was the first day of the August 2019 vacation break. Saint Lazare was a big, modern train station; Honora pushed her way through the crowds of student vacationers laughing, talking, and greeting each other with the French double kiss on the check. They seemed to be traveling in small groups of close friends or dating couples. Honora would see them boarding her train; they went into the cars marked 2ème Classe. Some cliques from the Lycée Le Mun had taken these holiday hikes to party on the coast at Deauville or Honfleur, although Honora never did. Besides not being invited, she never had a choice of where to go for vacation. It was always to visit Grand-mère and Grand-père Riaux. On that particular train, there was only one first class car and the only passengers were Honora and an elderly couple. She was relieved to be alone—at least for the seventy-five-minute journey to her destination. There was a lot to think about. For sure.

There were two five-minute stops to drop off and collect passengers at Mantes-la-Jolie and Evreux. Nobody boarded, but some got off the train. She saw hundreds waiting on the platforms on the other side of the tracks, waiting for the train to Paris. Several employees at the cabinet lived in Mantes, and Honora tried to imagine their grueling commute every workday.

They look so tired and stressed. Do some of them riot with the yellow vests on the weekend? Is that why they are so exhausted? Please don't let Pierre and Nicole from the office see me on the train. I have to keep this quiet for now.

Multiple thoughts and worries ran on the ticker tape moving inside her head.

Her train car was very quiet, and Honora didn't realize she dozed off after the stop at Evreux. The couple moving around to collect their luggage woke her up just as the train slowed to a stop in front of the small, red-brick station at Bernay. She straightened her thick, brown ponytail and smoothed her hair before zipping up her light jacket. *My Aigle parka is perfect for today. I got lucky that the boutique had it in my size and on sale too.* She felt secure and dry, wrapped in her new purchase at the annual June sales. Honora was ready for a new life in Normandy.

It was exactly 7:45 a.m. on Thursday, August 1, 2019. She was the only passenger to get off the train at Bernay besides the elderly couple riding with her in first class. Several small families boarded there for the onward journey to Deauville/Honfleur. The couple patiently waited for Honora to exit the train car before them. She appeared nervous and in a hurry. When they saw her struggling with the last, big Longchamp tote, the husband took it down to her on the platform. It was raining lightly and about fifty degrees in Bernay. *It's still very early, and I'm sure the skies will clear up soon*, she thought.

Reality check: This was the first time Honora Favre traveled by herself on a train, and she just had assumed that, like in Paris, taxis would be abundant at the Bernay station. Wrong. When she slowly walked outside the station, packed like a mule and dragging two of the three Longchamp totes, no taxis, no buses! Nothing but village people parked along the curb in their small, weathered Peugeots, Renaults, or Citroens, looking for their arriving friends or family to come outside.

For a moment, Honora was dumbfounded. *How could I be so stupid? Thinking taxis will be everywhere like at home?* She was a bit frustrated with her naiveté and ineptitude. She heard a short honk and a woman's voice coming from the street in front. An old silver Peugeot van was slowing as it approached the station exit where Honora stood. She couldn't believe her *bon* chance!

Angelique, Grand-père's housekeeper, happened to catch a glimpse of Honora while driving past the *gare*.

Angelique LeNormand had known Honora for like forever! She had kept the guestrooms tidy for Honora and her parents every summer holiday when they stayed at the Riaux farm. She never, ever expected to see Honora in this location and in this condition, looking like a lost tourist with no place to go. Then she realized that she was going to miss out on the quiche her family was waiting for: "They will sell out of the quiche at Louise by the time I get there. But so be it. Just need to call the *boulangerie* early tomorrow to reserve one." Angelique's family looked forward to the freshly baked quiche from Boulangerie Louise. Most weeks, it was their typical Thursday lunch.

Angelique represented everything good about her Viking ancestors who raided and then settled those parts in the ninth century. She was a tall, large, robust redhead who loved to rise and shine before sunrise every day and tend to her brood and their menagerie of pets and livestock before she jumped in the shower to drive off to her day job—cleaning people's houses. Her entire life was family and work. She was only eighteen when she and Pascal took their wedding vows at the parish church in nearby Bourg-Achard. It was only ten minutes from her birth village, Flancourt. Angelique thrived being close to her roots. It couldn't have been any other way. Yes. She had graduated from the lycée in Bourg-Achard, as her parents insisted. But that was the extent of her formal education. She and Pascal were madly in love and determined to start their own family as soon as possible after the lycée.

Pascal's brother already had found him a decent- paying job at the John Deere dealership/garage in Pont-Audemer. The tractor business was on fire in that entire area, and they needed mechanics, tout de suite. As for Angelique, well, she didn't have a driver's permit yet for the simple reason that she never learned how to drive. But people liked and trusted her, and she was a good cleaner. In days, she had three large households to clean at ten euros per hour. The old *vélo* from a neighbor's junk heap would do for the time being. She bicycled to her house jobs every day in all kinds of weather for the first couple of years. No problem for a country girl. Her thick, fleshy legs were sturdy for pedaling down the narrow, dirt country roads. Once they found jobs, the young couple quickly asked their parents for help getting a mortgage to buy a small lot outside their village and began to build their home. Following the custom of native Normandy clans, their family relations and friends had all pitched in to do the foundation, wiring, and plumbing for the young couple's nest. At the age of forty-one, Angelique was in her prime. She was a credit to her Viking ancestors, physically and mentally.

In those seconds after her little utility van took the unexpected turn into the driveway of *la gare* Bernay, Angelique could sense that Honora needed help. She had sharp instincts. "Mademoiselle Favre, *quelle* surprise! Are you okay? Are you going to the Riaux house? Can I help you?"

As Angelique talked out her window, Honora felt so relieved to find her ride to Grand-père's that she just walked to the rear of the silver, dusty van and clicked the double doors open. Her luggage hit the inside of the van hard and heavy—like a bale of hay—and Honora quickly jumped in the passenger seat next to Angelique. *"Oui. Je suis en route pour la ferme. C'est gentil de me transporter, Angelique."*

It was well after 8 a.m., and Honora couldn't help worrying about her parents back at the apartment. *I hope that Maman doesn't panic and call the police, and I hope Papa is not too angry. Should I call them now or send a text to Maman?* The truth was that the tumbler of Calvados downed by Chantal the night before had knocked her out for several hours. She still felt doped up when the light came through the blinds in their bedroom around 7 a.m., so she limped to the toilet and then let herself fall back onto the bed and keep dreaming. Calvados was a home remedy, of sorts, in the old Normand households. As a child, Chantal Riaux Favre had seen her elders use it for various ailments, including insomnia, anxiety attacks, or just plain, everyday stress. The shock and panic that had swelled up in Chantal during Honora's revelations had driven her to down the Calvados—a desperate act of which the lawyer in her felt ashamed. Her husband was a heavy sleeper and didn't move a muscle. They were both in a deep slumber while their girl embarked on her adventure.

The ride from Bernay to the Riaux farm outside Bonneville-Aptot was about forty-five minutes. Angelique had never had close personal contact with Honora before this. She could smell her clean, freshly shampooed hair. *It's Kerastase gold label. Expensive. Did she bring the bottle in her luggage? She won't find it anywhere out here in the boonies.*

Angelique could sense that Honora was more mature than last year and that she was on some kind of mission or in some kind of trouble. But, of course, out of respect for her longtime patron, Monsieur Riaux, she didn't dare ask Honora any questions and concentrated more than usual on her driving as they swerved left and right through the narrow, winding roads.

After half an hour or so, Angelique's van cleared the rolling hills and valleys after the small town of Bernay in route to the farm. The bright Normandy sun pushed through the clouds as they approached Bonneville-Aptot, the tiny village just before the turn-off to Grand-père's.

Honora had forgotten how clean and crisp the air was on the Bonneville plateau. It was no more than five hundred feet above sea level, but the purity of the air was almost like being in the Alps. And when you looked upward, the skies were spectacular and fast-changing. The heavens above Aptot had not changed since Monet, Matisse, and Renoir set up their easels here to paint them.

It was a veritable rural paradise—a world of endless fields of growing wheat, linen, corn, and sugar beets; apple orchards; and emerald-green pastures with fat, blonde, happy cows. Humans somehow were secondary beings in these parts—mere stewards of nature. Strange that Honora felt like she was coming home because Paris had always been home.

Angelique instinctively signaled and turned right onto the long *chemin de gravier* leading to Grand-père's red-brick home. It was not a typical farmer's house. Au contraire, it was a two-story maison de maître or mansion house thoroughly modernized with triple-glazed windows, a terracotta tile roof, marble walk-in shower, and la pièce de résistance, an immense, American-style island kitchen equipped with a La Cornue range and a Siemens double-sided refrigerator/freezer. The new kitchen had been a 2010 welcome home gift to Honora's Grand-mère, Audrey-Marie, following her long hospital stay in Rouen. Sadly, her remission from intestinal cancer was short-lived. She was taken from Grand-père only two years later.

A wave of peace and joy came over Honora when Veronique stopped in front of the house. She was on the right path. *Grand-père will be happy to see me even if it is a surprise. He will know what to say to Maman and Papa. That's it. I will wait for him to phone them first.* Her thoughts eased her guilty conscience about how she had lied to her parents on their last evening together.

CHAPTER 5

Normandy

Old Maurice Riaux was in his seventh year as a widower. He expected the time remaining for him in this life would be lonely and uneventful, except for his work. He would never give up running the farm— now a behemoth year-round operation—with his son, Eric, and his grandson, Bruno. In his youth, he stood nearly six and a half feet tall with a large, square head sitting on muscle-bound shoulders and biceps like a lumberjack. He always kept his red hair short and wore a gimme cap to protect his very fair skin from the Normandy sun and wind.

Despite his advanced age in the summer of 2019, his small, light- blue eyes remained clear, bright, and alert. With his new prescription glasses, Maurice could see for miles across his fields. The Normand genes were pure and strong in Maurice, and he had passed them on to Eric and young Bruno. But the younger generations were of more moderate builds. They had grown up in a modernized farming era when the combines, tractors, and bins did most of the work. Nevertheless, the three generations of Riaux farmers contended with year- round tilling, fertilizing, treating, planting, harvesting, and processing their domain of eight hundred acres. On days the weather did not cooperate, the long days ran into late nights of relentless labor. Mother Nature ruled this business, and the Riauxs knew how to read her and obey her commands to make a good profit every year.

That cloudy August morning, octogenarian Maurice was out in his far-west fields supervising one of their New Holland TC5 combine harvesters that Bruno Riaux, twenty-eight years old, was driving. Bruno had ridden inside a combine cab since he was knee-high, and driving these monsters was second nature to him. Of course, none of the Riauxs of Bonneville-Aptot had a clue that, while they worked their fields, a beautiful, young Parisian refugee was moving into Grand-père's house. Unannounced and uninvited.

As soon as Bruno saw his grandfather's expression while on his phone, he knew something was not right. Was it his parents? Or some problem at the other fields being harvested? Bruno couldn't stop the combine mid-field, so he carried on as he saw Maurice, phone still at his ear, hotfoot it back to his new, white Peugeot Partner van and take off.

Chantal was the first to awaken and go into the kitchen to brew her cup of Nespresso. She was careful not to wake Jacques. He works so hard and needs to just turn off the stress for the next few weeks. She was protective of her husband and worried about the level of tension that he faced at the law firm and in court. No sign of Honora. The door was ajar when she checked her daughter's bedroom. The bed was made, as usual, but when Chantal walked into the bathroom, it hit her. Honora had cleared out all her toiletries, makeup, and hairdryer, and her walk-in closet looked ransacked!

Chantal Favre had not completely gotten the Calvados out of her bloodstream from the night before, although it was past 10 a.m. Somehow, she could not believe what she saw before her: Honora's clothes and personal items were gone.

C'est pas vrai! Où est-elle? C'est ça—elle est partie pour la ferme. Chantal retrieved her phone from the salon where she had forgotten it during the scene with Honora and instinctively dialed her father, Maurice. In her mind she felt certain that the wise old man would know what to do to bring her back home to Paris if Honora had run away to his farm.

Maurice's conversation with his daughter was alarming and brief. His only granddaughter had been fired from the law firm. Last night, she had announced that she no longer wanted to live in Paris. Not ever. She was moving to Normandy permanently. Chantal suspected that Honora had run away to the Riaux farm, and she wanted Maurice to find her immediately. The call from his daughter ended abruptly because Maurice was illegally on a phone call while driving. He did not want to face the five hundred euros fine if a gendarme sighted him.

Audrey always took care of family squabbles, and I wish she were here! This is not my problem. Chantal and Jacques should come here to sort all this out with their daughter. But I can't simply throw my little flower out into the road. Honora has every right to stay here as long as she needs. She is a Riaux, after all, and this is a home for my people. The important thing is to find out what's bothering her and put her back on the right track. So many thoughts ran through his head. Maurice tried to reason it out and find a solution as he sped in his little van back to the house at Bonneville-Aptot. It was nearly lunchtime. He was worried and hungry.

"Bonjour, Grand-père! I took the first train to Bernay this morning, and Angelique drove me here. Have you any news from my parents? Has Maman called you?" Honora was full of excitement and questions as she greeted old Maurice with a big kiss on his sagging, leathery cheeks. It was a lip-gloss-sticky kiss, but he melted with relief and joy to see his *poupée*. Although his cutie pie was no longer the little tot who ran through his orchards. Kissing Maurice was a shining star of a woman. A young Riaux from Paris on an important mission.

Honora felt the same security, love, and warmth that she felt all her life when she was in that house. Unconditional love and acceptance. She felt the same wave of emotions that she had always felt from her grandparents, Audrey-Marie and Maurice. It was something primordial. She was sure that Grand-père would allow her to stay in the upstairs guest room. She was so sure that the elegant runaway had unpacked and arranged all her things in the closet and the guest bathroom before Maurice got to the house.

August was the height of tomato season, and Honora had forgotten how ruby-red, juicy, and sweet Grand-père's crop always was. His tomato hothouse was assembled in early May to plant and stake the six-inch-tall saplings in the special, black soil needed for fast sprouting. They were in the kitchen when she saw Grand-père take out a stale baguette from the breadbox and a wedge of Pont l'Évêque cheese from the larder next to the kitchen. Honora suddenly realized that this was her grandfather's typical lunch now that he was alone.

She put her hand lovingly on old Maurice's shoulder and told him, "*Attendez Grand-père, je vais chercher des tomates et faire une salade avec d'oignons et vinaigrette. Où sont les oeufs?*" Tomato and onion salad with a vinaigrette and a whipped omelet of farm fresh eggs: this she knew how to do! She briskly walked to the hothouse and, in minutes, returned to the kitchen with four perfectly ripe tomatoes and began cutting them into bite-sized pieces together with two huge yellow onions, soil still clinging to the stalks.

Her mind and heart flooded with loving, fun memories as Honora prepared the delicious concoction: How wonderful that I remember where all the pots and pans are kept, and the knives too. Nothing has changed from when I was a little girl watching Grand-mère do the same things I am doing today! It's like I never left this old place. Honora was building up confidence as she threw together a quick, delicious lunch for Maurice. While she was chopping the tomatoes, he motioned to the sideboard holding the big ceramic bowl of eggs collected this morning from the *poulailler*. Maurice had designed and built his own chicken coop, and he was proud of it. It kept over a dozen chickens and a rooster, producing huge brown eggs. The sturdy structure was invulnerable to the various local predators like foxes, hawks, and owls.

Honora loved that the eggs still had some feathers stuck on the shells and were warm. When she broke them into the cast-iron skillet with sizzling butter, their yolks were bright orange, as she remembered, and some had double yolks. The aroma rising from the skillet to fill the tiny kitchen was mouth-watering. While Honora flew around the kitchen, from the stove to the table to the sink to the larder, her subconscious was in full gear. It reminded her of an adage repeated among the womenfolk at family gatherings: the best way to a man's heart is through his stomach.

Grand-père never expected that he would be sitting down that day in his own kitchen to eat an impromptu, home-cooked lunch. Least of all that it would all be prepared by la petite, as he and his wife always called their only granddaughter. It was a bittersweet moment for the old farmer because, in his memory, he could see his life companion, Audrey-Marie, in their kitchen as he watched Honora cooking and serving that day.

They sat down on the rickety wooden chairs with woven-straw seats at the kitchen table and devoured it all—including the stale baguette, which didn't seem so stale after all.

"*C'est bon, très bon, ma chérie,*" Grand-père said as he began to dig into the hot omelette and delicious salad. "Of course, you can stay here, my dear, no problem at all. Your grandmother would be happy for you to keep me company at the farm as long as you need. Remember that you have always been our *petit chou.*" His eight decades of life taught Maurice many things, including patience. Sitting at his table, looking across at his granddaughter, he was sure that time was the best remedy for her misfortunes. Time was what Honora needed. Not chastisement, therapy or recriminations from him or her parents. No. She needed time to find herself and heal her wounds. And Normandy was the best place for her to be at this moment.

As it happened, Eric Riaux was in a quandary. A new, unexpected investment had literally been handed to him in the past few weeks that he did not have the time nor the inclination to deal with. A short-term loan to an old school friend who owned a restaurant nearby had not been repaid. His friend had moved away in financial straits and had signed papers transferring full ownership to Eric of his Restaurant de la Tour—lock, stock, and barrel. It included a furnished dining room with fourteen rectangular tables that could each seat up to six diners and a fitted, commercial-grade kitchen. It was in a sturdy *maison à colombage* with a generous cellar and a spacious, covered terrace, which even included a small apartment on the upper floor. The village known as Le Bec-Hellouin was full of these half-timbered,

Normand-style structures. Some dated back to the eleventh century when a knight-errant-turned-monk named Herluin—later called Hellouin—founded a humble abbey nearby.

Tourist sites on the internet rated Le Bec among the most charming villages in the whole Eure department—one of the ninety-four administrative subdivisions comprising the nation of France. That was an understatement. Le Bec-Hellouin—its official name—was nothing short of a fairy tale. Ensconced in a small valley naturally irrigated by a running, sparkling, cold-water stream called Le Bec, this place was a magnet for tourists and even rich Parisians looking for a weekend getaway. Some visitors never left and dispensed fortunes to restore the picturesque colombage houses or commission local builders to reproduce modern copies of the quaint habitations. Outside of the summer tourist season, Le Bec was a village with barely six hundred permanent residents. A whimsical locus where Rumpelstiltskin might live—a place that time forgot.

The crowning glory of the village was Herluin's present-day abbey with its bell tower, church, chapel, cloisters, and other complementary structures inhabited by Benedictine monks in 2019. The expansive collection of buildings, all constructed originally with manual labor using pure-white stone, echoed the enormous wealth and ecclesiastical power that Herluin's religious brotherhood accumulated by the eleventh century. As spiritual advisers to the Duke of Normandy, who after the Battle of Hastings in 1066 became William the Conqueror of England, Abbots Lanfranc and Anselm wielded subtle yet immeasurable influence in France and in England throughout that epoch. Both were to occupy the exalted position of archbishop of Canterbury, thanks to the goodwill and trust of the newly crowned king. William never forgot his Normandy roots. The glory days of the abbey and its monks came to a bloody and tumultuous end with the French Revolution. The immense holdings of the abbey were confiscated by the state. As government property, the buildings and grounds were used by Bonaparte as a breeding and training facility for the thousands of war horses sacrificed in his endless military campaigns. After the abbey fell into near ruin and was vandalized, burned, and plundered by succeeding generations, the French government in 1948 allowed it to once again become a place of worship and to be a home and workplace for a new holy order of monks.

Flowers grew in abundance around Le Bec and bloomed everywhere from April to September. Growing wild along the country roads of Le Bec and even popping up in the smallest alleys in the village, blood-red roses, poppies, primroses, anemones, bluebells, cowslips, trumpets, and other flowers were there for the picking. No fertilizer, no irrigation, no pruning. Le Bec dwellers never bothered to plant their flower beds or window boxes. The hundreds of bird species native to Upper Normandy scattered flower seeds virtually in every direction of Le Bec. These seeds then sprouted and bloomed a magnificent array of flowers every year.

The day after she arrived at the farm, Honora received a conciliatory text from her mother that there was good news from Maurice and everyone agreed that she could stay for a while. *Ma fille chérie, Grand-père m'a dit que tout va bien à la ferme et il est content que tu restes pour un court séjour. Papa et moi, nous sommes d'accord. Nous t'embrassons si fort. Bisous.* Honora felt relieved that her parents were accepting her new path. She finally found the courage to phone Maman. Their conversation was short, and Jacques Favre was not part of the call. *Is Papa angry at me and freezing me out of his life?* Honora wondered. But the tenderness and sincerity in Chantal's voice were reassuring. *I will call Papa in a few days. Give him time to calm down.* Honora didn't want another unpleasant confrontation. Long distance. What she wanted was to get on with her new life in Normandy.

Just as one door slammed shut on Mademoiselle Favre, a new and more enticing door miraculously opened. That evening, Eric Riaux appeared at the farm to welcome his wayward niece from Paris. His father had informed Eric of Honora's surprise arrival at the farm and that she was in urgent need of employment.

"It will not be easy to get the restaurant up and running. Do you know anything about managing an eating establishment? Do you know about taking reservations, greeting, handling diners, and cleaning up the tables quickly? Can you keep track of cash and credit card receipts and make a tally at the end of the night? Luc Carton has agreed to stay on as chef de cuisine—plenty of *savoir faire* there. But he is a tyrant in the kitchen, short fuse, you know." Eric was blunt with

Honora and cautioned her. He had not seen his niece in years and considered Honora a rich, somewhat spoiled kid. But he reminded himself that she was, after all, one-half Riaux, his sister's child, intelligent, well-bred, and well-educated, and that she had handled herself well at the Favre cabinet. Until she got fired.

"Uncle, you can count on me to manage your restaurant. Maman and Papa will tell you that I was a hard worker at the cabinet. They never found fault with my work, and I suspect that they disagreed with the way la Paul treated me and the others. The clients and my coworkers all liked me. Everyone except la Paul, that is. She had it in for me from the start. And I think I know the reason, and I will prove it someday. Give me a chance in Le Bec. You will not be sorry."

With a little prodding from Grand-père, Uncle Eric agreed to a three-month trial run at managing the restaurant and making it profitable. The bi-weekly salary was modest, but Honora counted on getting the 10 percent profit-sharing as soon as she got the place operating in the black. She was sure that she could do it.

Trial by fire. That's what it was. On the early morning of Saturday, August 3, Honora's uncle met her at the door of the restaurant, handed her the front and back door keys, gave a quick introduction to Chef Luc Carton, whose employment contract came with the restaurant, and then took off. She would clean up and open the following day—Sunday. There was no time to lose; the busiest tourist days in France were upon them. Carton had the kitchen fully operational, and he didn't hesitate to make clear to Honora that he was the top boss—chef—in his kitchen. Great. One less thing to worry about if he runs everything in there. Honora was relieved to be working with a seasoned pro.

Unbeknownst to Honora, Grand-père was keeping Chantal and Jacques *au courant* of their daughter's activities. They were thrilled and thankful for what they heard about the restaurant and offered to cover the salary for a waitress to help Honora and give her a fighting chance at her new venture.

Old Grand-père knew the perfect one for the job and, of course, promised not to say anything about who was actually paying for the waitress. Véronique LeNormand was seventeen years old and eager to make a little money until she returned to school in September. Honora was relieved. If she is Angelique's daughter, she will be a good worker. Anyway, I can't manage the restaurant alone. I need her to wait and clean up tables.

If Viking women could be beautiful, Véronique was at the front of the line. Large, tall, and robust with thick, strong arms and ankles like her mother, arctic-blue eyes, and of course, full, wavy red locks. She caught the frizzies on humid days. But so did most of her other Normand girlfriends. They didn't have the time to fret over their hair. They were kept busy with school and their daily assigned chores at home.

From ancient times in the ninth century when the family's savage ancestors arrived from Scandinavia to raid and then settle and populate northwestern France, boys and girls in the clans always helped with the family chores. It was an integral part of Viking culture. Children helped as soon as they could walk, picking up branches for tinder, hauling buckets of water from the streams, and trapping and hunting wild game—boar, rabbits, or deer—in the forests. Girls learned the art of building a wood fire, skinning, butchering, and roasting sanglier, lapin, or chevreuil, and picking and preserving wild berries and mushrooms that grew in abundance in the forests, fields, and even along roads. And, of course, doing laundry on the big, sharp rocks along the community stream or river.

The LeNormands were not rich by Parisian standards, but in their village—Illeville-sur-Montfort—they were among its most prosperous and respected citizens. Their two-level family house was new and modern, although modest in size. It looked much bigger than its actual size because of the eggshell-colored stucco with which its concrete block walls were coated.

Probably the most impressive feature of the LeNormand house was its unique location. Its entire west boundary, more than 350 feet long, ran along the majestic Montfort Forest, originally dedicated and protected by the crown of France in the thirteenth century. The great forest covered just under five thousand acres with towering pines, elms, oaks, and tilleuls—a species of linden tree.

Pascal LeNormand, Véronique's father, was proud to serve on the tiny commune's conseil administrative, village council. He took his civic duties seriously. Like his wife, Pascal believed in a strong work ethic for every member of his family. "*Bon! Félicitations, ma jeune. Bon courage au restaurant et occupe-toi bien de ton argent.*" His middle child was a self-starter already, and he congratulated her and warned her to safeguard her job earnings.

"*C'est incroyable, Véronique!* It is already the twentieth of August, and we are still fully booked until the very end of vacation!" Honora had passed her trial by fire in running the restaurant. Passed with highest honors. For more than two weeks, the unlikely threesome—Honora, Luc Carton, and Véronique—had pitched in together to successfully operate the Restaurant de la Tour.

Eric Riaux and Grand-père were speechless at how the Paris runaway was handling the business. Seeing the frenzy of work to be done six days a week, Eric relented and provided a young boy from his farm to come and help with the table clearing and the dishes. Honora's little team worked two lunch sittings and two dinner sittings. The online reservations were exploding, and the customer reviews posted on Yelp and other sites were five stars. None of the Riauxs, including Honora herself, could process just how fast the restaurant's business was growing. And it was because of the chef.

Many wrote that the nouvelle Normandie cuisine by Luc Carton was the most creative, exciting trend in a long time. Even the food critic for Paris's Le Figaro drove three hours to Le Bec to find out what all the fuss was about. Chef Carton did not disappoint. He was a native Normand, boastful and proud of the local, fresh, organic fruits and vegetables and a fanatic for the grass-fed beef from Normandy cows. He only cooked day-catch fish and shellfish from the nearby Cotentin Peninsula. All the wonderful varieties on his cheeseboard were unpasteurized, were rich with probiotics, and burst with delicious aroma and flavor. Being from Normandy, Carton knew that only dairy cows grazing in the emerald grasslands of the Le Bec Valley or nearby at Pont l'Évêque produced cheese good enough for his menus.

Coming from a household where Papa was king, Honora quickly learned how to handle Luc Carton's quick temper and very fragile ego. He was a Pavarotti in his kitchen. One night a Paris diner refused to eat the steaming bowl of mussels from Le Havre, claiming that they were too small and dry. The diner was the host of a large table. His guests also began to complain about the mussels.

Honora overheard the fuss at Véronique's assigned table. She was acquainted with such people. They were from her world. Rich snobs who liked to venture out of Paris to regions *moins raffinés*—primarily to remind themselves how superior and sophisticated they were. Parisians who gloated over less refined country folk for their entertainment. Poor Véronique, carrying the heavy ceramic bowl full of rejected mussels, meekly returned it to the kitchen. BAM! The cantankerous chef threw the bowl, which flew like a football, across the kitchen and crashed loudly against the back wall, falling to the floor in tiny pieces along with dozens of hot, wet mussels. Silence from the inside dining rooms and the tables on the terrace.

"*Je suis en panique!* And just what are we going to do now, Véronique?" Honora's face was red with panic when she ran into the kitchen and saw the mess; she was close to tears.

"He's an asshole. My mussels are superb," Chef Carton yelled and waved his hands, lambasting the diner who dared to complain about his mussels. Of course, he was heard throughout the restaurant.

Véronique whispered something to Honora as they crouched on the wet floor, quickly trying to clean up the mess of the mussel football. She silently nodded to Véronique and smiled. The table of the complaining diners all clapped as Véronique strutted out carrying a silver bucket of chilled Veuve Clicquot Brut Yellow Label with iced champagne flutes. Honora followed closely behind her and announced to the group that it was on the house and that the chef sent his apologies for any inconvenience with the food.

By the time the two women returned to the kitchen to check on Carton, his anger had subsided, and he was busy putting the finishing touches on the next order—a main course dish of *agneau de pré-salé origine Mont Saint-Michel.* He muttered, "Now let the idiots dare complain about this masterpiece."

CHAPTER 6

Philippe

The fatigue was blinding. Honora worked six days and nights per week—often more than twelve hours straight. The demands for tables on the phone and on the internet reservation site were unrelenting. It never let up, even though the August vacation break was nearly over. The Facebook page and Instagram account that Véronique had cleverly created for Restaurant de la Tour, Le Bec-Hellouin, Normandy, was exploding with more friends and followers every day. People loved the photos of Chef Carton's Normandy culinary creations. They drove from as far as Chartres and Le Mans to savor them.

Honora's parents were among the first Facebook friends for the restaurant. They couldn't believe their daughter's success and determination. True to her word to Uncle Eric, the restaurant was operating with a sizable profit. And Honora reaped the benefits. She was paid 10 percent of the gains on top of her base salary. She was so busy that going shopping or out for a *salade niçoise* and Perrier like she did with Sandrine in Paris never entered her mind. It was way too full of details and plans for the next day's menus, seating arrangements, supplier deliveries, and keeping a steady rein on Chef Luc. The extra bonus Eric paid him every week kept his temper tantrums under control.

Although the restaurant was transferred to Uncle Eric with ongoing supply contracts for the meat, fish, dairy products, and produce delivered daily to Chef Carton's kitchen, his obsession with serving only same-day-catch fish and shellfish was proving to be problematic. The supplier had to drive in the dark morning hours from the fishing boats at Barneville-Carteret, nearly at the farthest point of the Cotentin Peninsula. It took more than two hours to drive from the port to the restaurant, provided that there were no accidents on the motorway and the weather cooperated.

It was the final week of the August vacation break, and today—Sunday—was going to be a crazy day. The reservation internet site had overbooked for lunch and dinner—double-booked actually. Preparing for the onslaught, Honora rose at 6 a.m. Actually, she had been disturbed by an early-morning text from the fish-loading boss at Barneville. Véronique, too, seemed a little more on edge than usual; she arrived well in advance of her usual punch- in time for the lunch shift, 10 a.m. She wanted to make sure that Mademoiselle and the chef understood that she was returning to classes the following week and would no longer be helping at the restaurant.

Honora felt adrift knowing that Véronique—her right hand for everything—was leaving. She was also sinking, mentally and physically, from the prolonged weeks of nonstop work at the restaurant. The days and weeks seemed to blur into one interminable nightmare of duties and deadlines, and sometimes, Honora wasn't quite sure what day it was. She didn't like the text from Barneville. A new man would be collecting the restaurant order off the boats and making the delivery—Philippe. The fish-loading boss's regular man had been arrested last night in Le Havre. He was rioting with the yellow vests.

This bit of news was not communicated to Luc Carton. Why worry him or trigger another tantrum? His fish will be delivered on schedule, as always. Surely, they will send a reliable person. I need to see that the lower- level cellar loading door is open for this Philippe. Honora was thinking clearly while going through her checklist, preparing for the lunch shift. She felt better about the double-booking since setting up six additional tables on the outside terrace. The red umbrellas served as a huge, festive canopy over the terrace. An explosion of color with the lime-green resin chairs. The Métro BFMTV on Channel 15 forecasted a calm, sunny day. Ideal for dining on the terrace. Its earthen floor was covered with white- granite pebbles, which stayed cool in hot weather.

It was twenty minutes before opening time, and no fish! Honora's frantic texts to the fish boss were being ignored. She decided to go down to the cellar entrance and stand in the alley to wave down the driver whenever he showed up. Her phone was in hand, waiting for some news, anything, to confirm the order was on the way. Nothing. Before going down to wait outside, she had to update Chef Luc on the complication. He now scurried around in the kitchen, arranging the sauté and roasting pans, and he was irritated about *le 'petit' problème de la livraison du poisson.*

The first reservations arrived and were seated by 11:55 a.m.—five minutes before the lunch service was expected to begin. Inside the dining salons, Véronique chatted with the first customers, doing her best to stall. Thankfully, they all ordered aperitifs—tasty, sweet drinks like champagne or Schweppes agrumes to stimulate the appetite.

Ahh! This will give us a few more minutes for the fish to arrive . . . I pray that it does!

Véronique flashed a reassuring smile with her big mouth filled with perfectly straight, large white teeth. Her coral lipliner and lip tint were holding up okay, but she felt drops of sweat on her upper lip. Discreetly, she wiped it with the hem of her white apron.

The dirty blue refrigerator truck finally turned into the tiny alley. Honora saw it and let out a huge sigh of relief. It was 12:13 p.m.—the lunch service was in full swing. Véronique had started to take seafood orders from hungry diners. It was on the day's menu, and she had no choice. The chef was livid. Down in the alley, Honora watched the truck driver park and operate the controls to the loading platform. As he jumped down from the driver's seat, he glanced at Honora for a second and gave a "Bonjour!" with a slight nod.

"*Mon Dieu, Monsieur! Vous êtes vraiment en retard! Dépêchez-vous!*" Despite her nerves, Honora's tone with the driver was not squeaky or whiny. She didn't hold back that he was really late and asked him to hurry. She spoke from her throat in a smooth, assertive manner. Yet, it was feminine and sultry. It was the voice of a young woman in charge. Not a rich, coddled girl from Paris.

Honora had her head down, focusing on her Samsung tablet to check off the delivery. As she tried to concentrate on checking the items quickly before the crates were taken to the kitchen, her heart and her mind went into overdrive:

Fifteen total iced crates—thirty kilos;

Five langoustines;

Two oysters;

Three mussels;

Two salmon;

Three sea bass, trout, and turbot.

When she finally looked up from her list, she took notice of the new delivery guy. *He's gorgeous. Hot. Is this his regular job? Will he come back to do Tuesday's delivery? Probably not. He doesn't look nor speak like a real delivery guy.*

Nope. She guessed right. Philippe Thouroude was certainly not a real delivery guy. He was a twenty-nine-year-old Parisian—just graduated from Université Paris-Saclay—taking a summer break before starting his job at Vinci. While Honora was looking down at his tablet, signing to confirm delivery, he was all eyes on her.

His expression was that of a toddler seeing the Eiffel Tower Christmas light show for the first time. Ecstasy. It lasted only seconds. As soon as Honora looked up, the serious, business-like expression returned to his face. He knew she was upset about the delay. In fact, Honora was more than upset. She was furious at the shoddy handling, but she said nothing more to him except a quick, *"Merci. La livraison mardi, c'est bien prévu?"*

"Oui, Mademoiselle Favre, c'est prévu mardi. Je m'en charge. Je suis désolée pour le retard." Her signature was legible, and now he knew her name! Of course, Philippe was taking charge of the Tuesday delivery and he was glad that he kind of apologized for today. He couldn't wait to see this goddess again. Weird that I find this beauty way out here in the sticks. Is she from around here? Don't think so. Those are not Viking legs or boobs. He couldn't stop thinking about her on the drive back up the coast. He was an engineer. Technical, logical, detached. It was out of character for Philippe to be out-and-out captivated by a girl he had only just met.

Honora's Sunday flew by, and she was grateful for her day of rest the next day. The restaurant closed on Mondays, and she typically went in with Véronique to do some cleaning and organization work that was impossible to do on open days. But that last Monday of the August season, she texted Véronique not to come to the restaurant. Honora decided to take her first real day of rest since she came to Normandy. She slept late. Until 10 a.m.

Did she dream of the delivery guy? Absolutely. Philippe was in her most vivid dreams the night before and even into the early dawn hours after she got up to use the toilet and then went back to bed. She had never before had dreams so full of luscious, wet, sticky kissing, fondling, and touching. Being a virgin, her subconscious could not produce dreams of actual sexual relations. But it was enough for now. Plenty.

Honora had never experienced such sexual intensity, such yearning, for anyone. *Is this normal? To feel this raw, powerful, animal attraction to a man I barely know? To dream about doing stuff with him?* Honora felt a little ashamed and scared about her wild thoughts or feelings or whatever they were about Philippe. She was missing the company of her friend, Sandrine, who had experience in these delicate matters.

Their meeting had lasted only minutes, but she remembered everything about him. Oozing with a masculine aura, he smelled of fresh perspiration and aftershave—Hugo Boss, she guessed. Philippe's voice was definitely baritone, and his tone was friendly but assertive. He had smooth yet strong hands with very clean, manicured nails. Although his brown eyes were small, his eyebrows and eyelashes were dark and thick. Honora was taken with Philippe's obviously professional coiffure. Despite being cut short, it separated into tiny ringlets along his forehead and the back of his neck.

In her dreams, he was not wearing the company parka from last Sunday—he had only a fitted, long-sleeve T-shirt, navy blue. She could see Philippe's thick biceps and flat abs flex each time he unloaded the heavy seafood crates.

Honora's mind was swimming with questions and misgivings: I should have brought my Dolce and Gabbana pencil skirt with the black lace top. There is nothing here good enough to wear tomorrow. Only work slacks with tops, and most of them are stained from the restaurant. What am I going to do about shoes? I have nothing but beat-up flats here! As Honora did for the law firm job, her nightly ritual included planning her wardrobe for the following day. This was very different, though. She was dressing for him, after all. She had to be a knock-out.

Luc Carton was an extremely high-strung individual. A male prima donna—a veritable Pavarroti. He insisted on being present when Tuesday's seafood delivery arrived. Allegedly, Sunday's order was incomplete— there was no turbot at all in any of the marked crates. There was no way Honora could refuse. Chef Carton had every right to inspect the seafood as it was unloaded. Philippe arrived at 8 a.m. on Tuesday. Slightly earlier than expected. Honora was already outside the cellar delivery door, waiting. She was dressed to the nines with the most perfect blowout of her thick, shoulder-length hair and maquillage— pretty yet not overdone, sexy yet not vulgar, chic yet not extravagant.

But just as Philippe started unloading, Chef Carton strutted down the cellar steps toward the truck. *"Bonjour, Monsieur. Il n'y avait pas de turbot dans la dernière livraison. Merci d'établir un avis au bon montant."* Philippe nodded his assent and made a note on his tablet to issue a credit for the missing turbot in the last delivery, and then he offered the device to Honora for her signature. The rest of the delivery went well enough. Pavarotti was placated. Honora and Philippe tried to be subtle, but their attraction to each other was electric. All she could say as he jumped back in the truck was, *"Merci beaucoup, Monsieur. À bientôt."* She did not know then that Philippe would not return to make any deliveries.

It was not to be believed. The Favres of Paris and the Riaux clan of Normandy, being dominated by each of their paterfamiliases, had a hard time admitting it. Especially Papa. Their beautiful child, who was supposed to go to university, graduate, marry a wonderful boy from a good Parisian family, and settle down to raise her children in a grand residence in *la septième* had done none of that. Instead, she quit Paris while deceiving her parents and ran away to Normandy to live on a farm and manage a small, seasonal restaurant in the middle of nowhere. The icing on the *gâteau* was that Honora Favre succeeded. She succeeded in building a whole new and different life for herself at twenty-three years of age. Her father, more than all the others, remained firmly convinced that she would return to her life in Paris. Eventually. "We must be patient and allow Honora to go through her revolutionary period. She will return to Paris and live a proper life. You will see it happen, Chantal." Jacques repeated this mantra, of sorts, nearly every week when his wife brought up the subject of Honora and her life in Normandy. He was not the least bit concerned. Something in his gut told him that his daughter was headed in the right direction, that someday she would do something great and important for the family and that it would be in Paris. Favre was a man of hard facts, not fuzzy feelings or premonitions, so he kept such thoughts to himself.

Best of all, Honora's success transformed her parents' opinion of her. She was no longer a liability. A failing student with no place to go. They now saw the young woman as *très courageuse*, and they admired her courage and tenacity in taking the restaurant managing job and making it work. Chantal and Jacques began to respect their daughter as an independent adult and give her the freedom to live according to her wishes and goals—not their own. Honora was about to make dramatic changes to her life and lifestyle, which were extremely different from what Chantal and Jacques planned for her.

Twenty-nine-year-old Philippe Thouroude was beside himself. He lost the seafood delivery gig and couldn't think of a plausible excuse to show up at the Le Bec restaurant to see her. The Barneville delivery supervisor had reinstated his regular man, Youssef. After his arrest and detention for being a rioting yellow vest at the La Havre protests, he was released on bail. His union lawyer got the charges against him suspended, provided that the accused stayed out of trouble, including no traffic infractions, for the next twelve months. Philippe reminded himself that it was only a temporary job while staying with a family cousin, the Comtesse d'Osmoy, in an obscure hamlet called Aptot. It was just something to do before he began his career as a construction engineer. The Comtesse was an elderly widow who lived alone at Château d'Aptot, and she was enchanted to have a young person keep her company at the château. She enjoyed staying in touch with that side of the family; after all, Philippe's mother, Isabelle Amelia, was a Thouroude cousin. The young houseguest only planned to stay a few weeks. His employment contract at Vinci did not start until early October, and the Paris headquarters had not yet confirmed his first assignment. So, for the moment, Philippe was kind of a tumbleweed.

"*Oui! Bien sûr, Philippe. J'entendu dire que Maurice Riaux a une petite fille Parisienne qui habite chez lui à la ferme. Pour l'instant, elle gêre le restaurant Le Bec-Hellouin.*" Out of desperation for finding a way to see Honora again, Philippe had asked the Comtesse if she knew anyone working in the Restaurant de la Tour at Le Bec. But of course, she had heard talk about Maurice's Parisian granddaughter. The villages were in close proximity, and their inhabitants kept up to date on the comings and goings of the local families. Especially the big landowners like the Riauxs.

The Comtesse was a contemporary of Maurice, although they did not socialize on the same level. She read the young man's face as Philippe talked about Honora and asked questions. She understood. *He's smitten, for sure. I'll arrange some pretext to see Maurice, and Philippe can drive me over to the farm. We will go next Monday when the girl's restaurant is closed.* The old *châtelaine* figured it out.

The third Monday in September 2019 was an unusually cold, rainy day in Aptot. The Normandy summer had come and gone. The days were getting shorter. It was her day off, but Honora couldn't stay in bed when she heard Grand-père stirring in the kitchen, trying to get some breakfast. Her phone showed it was shortly after 7 a.m. She quickly showered and threw on her Jean-Paul Gaultier jeans and a lightly starched, white blouse from Boutique Anne Fontaine, with a cognac-colored thick sweater draped across her shoulders and tied loosely under her chin. The sweater set off her chestnut hair which she decided to wear loose. Honora wanted to feel and look casual today. *I'll give my face a rest today; no makeup, only a dab of moisturizer—pas de maquillage, un peu de crème.*

Today, Maurice was venturing out to the north fields to help his grandson, Bruno. The sugar beet harvest was finished; the soil needed to be worked and prepared for the next crop. Maurice would receive an unexpected call from the Comtesse d'Osmoy while out in the fields. The tractor noise made it difficult to understand what she was saying; he only made out that she was coming to the farm around noon. *"Oui, Comtesse, je serai heureux de vous accueillir à la ferme. A toute à l'heure."* Of course, Maurice couldn't refuse the lady's request for a visit; whatever she needed, he would keep it short. He called Honora and told her to clean up the kitchen table and set up the Nespresso coffee maker. A distinguished lady visitor was arriving around noon. Just to be sure, she should prepare to serve four people, including themselves. Maurice hadn't seen the

Comtesse drive herself for a long time, so he assumed someone would accompany the lady.

"Bien sûr, Grand-père, pas de souci." Honora assured her grandfather that this would be no problem. She already had picked up the breakfast things and sponged the vinyl tablecloth clean. Honora checked that the Nespresso water reservoir was full and that there was a variety of coffee capsules available to pop in. Then she opened her grandmother's cupboard and took out the Limoges coffee service—a complete service for fifteen. She noticed that everything in the cupboard was covered in a light layer of dust, so Honora decided to carefully wipe each and every piece of the fine porcelain with a damp, clean tea towel. As her hands carefully cradled each piece, she remembered the many happy times passed in that house. I love these old dishes, and I hope that dear Grand-mere up in heaven knows that we are using them today! It would be the first time the heirlooms were used since Audrey-Marie Riaux, née Ferry, took her last breath in her bedroom upstairs.

About two miles around the bend in the tiny hamlet of Aptot, the Comtesse heard the old longcase clock in the hallway strike twelve o'clock. She descended the tall, wooden staircase from her second-floor suite. Her steady, skeletal hand never loosened its grip on the brass banister; she knew that any misstep or slip on those stairs could be fatal at eighty-eight years of age.

She had discarded her widow's weeds years ago and wore a navy- blue dress trimmed with a white lace collar. She never was seen without her platinum

Cartier wedding band and her small pearl ear studs. She treasured the matched pair of south sea pearls because the marvelous natural oyster beds that produced them were extinct.

Her husband, the Comte d'Osmoy, was not to live a long life. A fatal aneurysm next to his aorta had taken him nearly twenty years before. She had placed his coffin under the ancient stone floor of the château's Église Saint-Jean-Baptiste d'Aptot. His final resting place was next to the remains of the Comte Thouroude, who was granted the immense domain—twenty-five thousand acres—in the seventeenth century by Louis XIII, king of France, and had constructed the first section of the ancient castle.

Philippe was a descendant of Thouroude, and for some strange reason, he went by this surname—his mother's family name—while he lived in Normandy. He concealed his real last name, his father's family name.

The Comtesse thought this was bizarre behavior for a young gentleman of his background, but she didn't question Philippe about it. When she went out of the tall, wooden, double doors of the château, Philippe was waiting for her. He stood by the passenger side of his 2018 Mini Cooper, and he held the door open for his distinguished host and extended his hand to help the old châtelaine board.

Bravo, Philippe! she silently cheered him. She was taken with the young cousin. Philippe drove very slowly around the deep gravel allée from the castle to the grande portail. The twenty-foot-high, solid-iron gate had been mechanized long ago. It opened automatically as the Mini approached. Once he had cleared the gate and was on the paved road to the farm, Philippe accelerated to fifth gear in seconds. It was a remote, nearly forgotten, niche in the Normandy countryside, and the road belonged to him alone. Philippe hoped that the Comtesse wouldn't hear his heart pulsating loudly inside his chest. It was out of his control.

They drove past the open gate to the Riaux farm, slowing down to a crawl. He didn't want his tires to catch any chickens or the rooster roaming in the front garden. It was 12:15 p.m., and Maurice Riaux came outside his maison de maître to greet the visitors. He rushed home earlier than planned to change into a pair of freshly laundered zipper overalls. Receiving a local member of nobility in his dirty work clothes was out of the question.

What could this old lady possibly want from me? Why did she propose to come to me instead of asking me to go to Aptot for this meeting? This doesn't smell right. Maurice's mind ran rampant with guesses about the object of the impromptu rendezvous requested by the Comtesse. He did not accumulate his wealth by having problems with neighbors. Especially not the important ones.

Honora knew the visitors were driving up to Grand- père's as soon as she heard him go out the front door and speak to someone. She hurried to check that the coffee service which she laid out for four people was clean and in good order and turned on the Nespresso machine.

She felt like the floor underneath had opened and swallowed her when she went into the reception salon. Tongue-tied for the first time in her life, she curtsied to the Comtesse. A ghost from her childhood, although a pleasant one.

"*Maurice et Honora, permettez-moi de vous présenter mon cousin, Philippe Thouroude. Il passe un court séjour avec moi au château avant de commencer sa grande carriere au sein de Vinci.*" The old noblewoman had made thousands of social introductions in her long lifetime, but this one, she sensed, was of epic proportions.

She turned to look at Philippe, and he was smiling and sweating simultaneously. *Embarrassing,* she thought. But she was not in a royal palace, only at a farmer's house with his granddaughter, so the Comtesse was not too put out by her cousin's strange demeanor. She noticed how Honora had matured since their last meeting, and she approved of the natural elegance and beauty the Riaux granddaughter had acquired.

Maurice ushered the visitors into the rustic formal dining room where Honora had arranged for serving coffee. Honora was the perfect hostess. "*Voudriez-vous un café, Madame La Comtesse? Et votre cousin?*"

Following protocol, Philippe remained silent while the Comtesse told Honora that they both would be taking a simple black coffee. "*Nous voudrions tous les deux du café noir, s'il vous plait, sans sucre. C'est très gentil de nous accueillir au dernier minute, Maurice.*"

The grand old lady wasn't born yesterday; she easily picked up on what was going on between the young male Thouroude and the Riaux granddaughter. So, while Honora prepared the coffee in the kitchen, the Comtesse casually chatted with Maurice about needing his advice for some diseased tilleuls on the castle grounds. What did he advise her to do? Prune them severely to excise the fungus or remove them altogether? She was accomplished at the practice of artifice and manipulating the male ego. This was France, after all.

She is even more beautiful than at the restaurant! Philippe thought as he stared at Honora. *Why does her face look younger than at Le Bec? I can't believe that I am actually here with her. Does she like me? How are we going to get together? Just the two of us. There isn't much time left before I must return to Paris.* Philippe's head was exploding with questions. When he finally picked up the cup of fine Limoges, the coffee was cold. He drank it anyhow. Rudeness or bad manners were out of the question. Especially here. Especially now.

Their eyes met during the elders' conversation, and they exchanged a few *merci beaucoups* and *s'il vous plaits*. Nothing more than that. To Honora, though, it felt like their hearts connected somehow, and she knew what was happening to her. She was falling in love with a man she barely knew. Or was it only a heady infatuation for an attractive stranger?

In keeping with the charade of coming to ask Maurice for advice, the visitors from Aptot couldn't prolong their visit past forty minutes. The Comtesse rose to her feet and thanked the farmer Riaux for his very kind indulgence and hospitality. Maurice replied,

"Avec plaisir, Madame la Comtesse, nous étions ravis de votre visite."

As they got back into Philippe's Mini, Honora came outside with her grandfather to say goodbye. She held a small basket that she had prepared with four red, plump tomatoes, which she passed to Philippe through the open car window and smiled. A jolt of electricity passed between them for an instant as he took the basket.

CHAPTER 7

Deauville

It was the time of year when the North Sea wind gusts from Scandinavia and the British Isles are seen crashing against the white, chalky cliffs of the Normandy coast. The resort towns along that scenic coastline, Deauville, Trouville, and Honfleur, were always chilly and windy in November and for several months thereafter. The 2019 Deauville winter was no exception. But that did not stop people from flocking there for pleasure.

F. Scott Fitzgerald and Ian Fleming had their immortal characters gamble and party in Deauville. It reeked of old and new money, entertainment, and history—akin to the American Newport, Rhode Island. Parisians who could afford it came often to Deauville—every weekend in the summer and most of August. Many kept magnificent villas in town, facing the sandy, white beach. These mansions, finished in the Normandy colombage style with terracotta roofs, were regularly rented in the winter season when families wanted to get away from the big cities and celebrate Christmas and the New Year together, *en famille*.

The coastline occupied by Deauville, Trouville, and nearby Honfleur was dubbed the Parisian Riviera since the 1800s, although surviving records indicate that this area had been strategically important to France for a very long time before. It was where William, who was at the time a mere duke of Normandy, visited his ally, le Seigneur Hubert de Canisy, to plan the mighty Battle of Hastings which made him William the Conqueror, king of England. That fateful rendezvous, somewhere on Mont Canisy high above Deauville, changed the course of history up to the present day, and some say the castle where that meeting took place still exists.

Perhaps because of the connection with William the Conqueror, British royalty and nobility long gravitated to this whole area. It was referred to as the Côte Fleurie, famous for its year-round display of colorful flowers, its horse racing, its sumptuous gambling casinos, and its virtually unlimited number of fine restaurants and gourmet delicatessens that served the best of local seafood.

Decades before Honora's fate took her to Deauville, the town's leaders decided to emulate the fame and fortune of the Cannes Film Festival in the south of France. Its chamber of commerce took the bold move of inaugurating and financing a Deauville American Film Festival. It was a phenomenal opportunity for new American films that didn't qualify for Cannes, as well as a fat cash cow for Deauville's merchants. By 2019, the Deauville Film Festival had been in full swing for forty-five seasons and rivalled its Cannes competitor. Moguls and other celebrities of the film industry flocked to the Festival every September.

That fateful wet and gray day in September when Philippe had come to Grand-père's farm with his cousin, the Comtesse, changed everything for Honora and for Philippe. It changed their lives in ways they never imagined possible. Philippe remained at Château d'Aptot while waiting for his first assignment from Vinci; he expected to hear from his new company any day. The couple began to see each other almost every day and for as long as possible.

Honora was touched that Philippe volunteered, actually insisted, on driving her to work and picking her up in his Mini every workday—six days a week. Honora was relieved to keep their dates mainly riding in Philippe's car. She was wild about him and feared what would happen if they were completely alone for an extended period. He kissed her with such passion and tenderness that it made her dizzy; her body wantonly reacted to their foreplay. His tongue had started to explore inside Honora's mouth and down her blouse to her nipples, and this was extremely arousing to her. Honora was discovering the powerful force of her sexual feelings.

Philippe always held Honora's left hand tightly in the car as he chatted her up about all his plans at Vinci. He was excited about starting his career at the big company and learning the tough business of building large, commercial facilities. He told her that it was his dream to one day be the founder and owner of a Vinci, operating on a global scale, not only in France.

September was nearly over when Philippe picked her up at 11 p.m. as Honora was locking the restaurant doors at Le Bec. "They called today. My first project is in Deauville—a new hotel and golf resort for the Barbot chain. I report to work next Monday, October seventh."

Both knew this was coming, but it was still hard to face. Separation. Although not saying it outright, both knew, deep in their hearts, that they were madly in love. For Honora, her feelings for this man were like a bomb of emotions exploding inside her: excitement, joy, passion, anticipation, and most of all, an overwhelming, primal desire to be with Philippe. To be with him day and night, rain or shine, good or bad, whatever the circumstances. Lying in bed at night at Grand-père's, Honora sometimes wondered if this was normal, if her mother had experienced this torrent of emotions with her father. She hesitated to confide so much of these new feelings and experiences to anyone, especially her mother.

Philippe's first weeks at Vinci were brutal. Still, he was ecstatic with doing his new job duties, meeting the people, reading architectural plans with the designers, and working with the boots on the ground that set up the heavy equipment to dig the foundation. Exhilarating to the ambitious, driven young man. It was like a fire burning inside Philippe, although he did not know how he came to feel this way about working and succeeding. Certainly not from his father.

He had taken a year lease for a one-bedroom, furnished condo in a large building next to the Deauville Yacht Club. He moved in literally twenty-four hours before he started work, and his possessions were two black duffle bags with wrinkled clothes, some old Nikes, his backpack with computer, a Braun razor, and a few toiletries. The condo wasn't much in size, but the monthly rent was reasonable, and it had a new kitchen and shower with a sweeping view of the sailboats anchored in the marina.

Driving to and from the Riaux farm and the restaurant on weekends to see his beloved was exhausting; Philippe was starting to worry about punching the clock too early at work each Friday when he sped off to see Honora. Mondays, Honora's day off, were impossible for Philippe. He was expected to be on-site from 7 a.m. to 7 p.m., five days a week. Many nights, he would lie awake in the condo, frustrated at their separation. They had been a couple since September, and he couldn't wait any longer. He had to take decisive action. Now.

Honora remained committed to running the restaurant at Le Bec and keeping her grandfather company at the farm. Some weekends, Véronique came to help out and make a few extra euros. She liked working with Mademoiselle Favre, as she would always call her. Honora liked the early hours of a farmer and the tranquility of the countryside. She didn't mind helping Grand-père with the small, daily chores, like collecting the day's eggs from the *poulailler* and feeding the rooster and his hens.

It was getting harder every time that she was with her Philippe. Their kisses, touching, and fondling over their clothes were intense and satisfying. But not enough. Philippe ejaculated inside his clothes a few times, which was embarrassing for both of them. Honora couldn't wait much longer to do what she yearned to do. To make wild, passionate, unfettered, hot *l'amour* with Philippe. She thought it premature to start birth control pills so soon after their first date. Although she felt an urgent need to talk to someone about what was happening to her. It was a prolonged FaceTime visit, but Sandrine spoke to Honora like a sister. She held nothing.back.

Years before, Honora had discussed some of these topics with Chantal. As mother-daughter discussions on that subject tend to be, their talks were distant and hypothetical. Now Sandrine was talking to Honora about "the real thing." It was scary and embarrassing. Safeguarding and respecting your body was at the top of Sandrine's list of dos, and she also had many *don'ts* to share with her innocent friend.

"Even after you are on the pill, he should use a condom. Attention. Be careful. Sometimes those things tear in the heat of passion. Remember what an unwanted pregnancy would do to both of your lives. Don't lose your head like I did with Richard."

Honora was grateful to Sandrine for talking to her so openly. But she did not pursue that last thing her friend said. About losing her head with Richard. That thought haunted Honora, and she prayed that she had been mistaken about Richard Lambert using Sandrine as a fresh, fast fuck. That forty-minute FaceTime visit hit Honora like a bolt of lightning. She was wading into the deep end of an ocean, for the first time and with no life jacket. But Honora was sure of one thing: this was her time to fall in love and cross the threshold of being a woman. Her physical desire, her hunger to be with Philippe in the most intimate way, felt perfectly natural.

They were in the Mini, driving from the restaurant to the Riaux farm. It was close to midnight when Honora had finally finished cleaning up with the busboy and was able to lock up. It would be the very early hours of Monday morning when Philippe rolled into his parking garage in Deauville.

He had rehearsed in front of his shaving mirror for several days before, but he was still nervous and rigid as they got closer to Grand-père's. At the last minute, he decided to stop on the side of the dark, empty road just before the turn to climb to the Bonneville-Aptot plateau. The right turn was at a run-down commune called Pont Authou—mostly public apartment housing apartments and a nursing home, totaling about two hundred inhabitants. The traffic light at the turn was flashing; there was no traffic at that late hour.

Honora turned to look at Philippe when he stopped the car and turned off the engine. She was a bit alarmed. Philippe had a serious, solemn expression and turned to look at her for a couple of seconds before he began to speak. "Ecoute, chérie." His tone was almost like that of a supplicant in church. As if he was about to plead or pray.

"We have not known each other very long—not even two months. And I understand that you are younger and somewhat inexperienced in life. But we cannot go on like this. Living in different places, and me rushing back and forth every weekend to be with you. It is not good for either one of us to continue this way. You must know by now that I am in love with you. Although you do not say it, I think you love me too. My feelings for you are the real thing. This is a big deal for me. Even if I live to be one hundred, I will never feel about another woman the way I feel about you now. That is not going to change. It is only logical and proper that you come to live with me in my condo at Deauville. Of course, you should keep your job in Le Bec. My situation with my parents is complicated. We both need to work things out with our parents, so they know what is happening. In due course, we should sort out our living arrangements and begin to plan our wedding. You belong to me. I will never allow you to be with any other man but me. Ever."

Honora's heart felt like it went into atrial fibrillation by the time Philippe finished talking. Thunderstruck, to put it mildly. She was not expecting this; his words were so final and demanding. Pont Authou had no streetlights, and the Mini's headlights were off. Except for the faint flash from the traffic light at the intersection, it was pitch- black on the tiny road. But she could see that Philippe had tears welled up in his eyes, and he looked abnormally pale. Her knee-jerk reaction was to grab his big, beautiful head and plant a long, hard kiss on his lips. She did this with all her might and with all the ferocious love she felt for him at that moment.

After the kiss, Philippe regained his composure and blurted out something Honora had already discovered but had kept to herself. "Before you say anything, you need to know my real name. Ferdinand Philippe Thouroude d'Orléans."

For the young lovers, things transpired quickly and unexpectedly in the final weeks of October and the beginning of November. By mid-November, when winter fully set into the Normandy coast, Honora and Philippe were living ensemble in Philippe's tiny condo overlooking the private marina of the Deauville Yacht Club. They were a "real" couple now; Honora was no longer a virgin. Shortly after her long FaceTime with Sandrine, Honora decided to start her birth control— low dose Loestrin pills like Sandrine was taking.

The first time for her was the most natural, erotic act that her body had ever engaged in. Magical and fulfilling. She had nearly reached the pinnacle of womanhood, and it was a new, extraordinary identity for Honora. She was somebody's *copine* or girlfriend now. Philippe was besotted with Honora, the first woman with whom he lived. He couldn't get enough of Honora—physically or emotionally. He liked to indulge her every whim, whether doing their grocery shopping or taking her old Land Rover for repairs. He doted on her to show his love.

She didn't mind the long drive on the A13 motorway to return to her job at Le Bec. Uncle Eric was not overly disturbed when he heard the shocking family news: his young, apparently innocent, Parisian niece was moving in with her boyfriend, Philippe. Money talks, and it said to Eric, in no uncertain terms, that he could not possibly fire Honora. The restaurant had a good cash flow under her management. Young people moved in together and were "living in sin" all the time. They had babies with no marriage to bind them.

Yet the Favres in Paris and the Riaux family at Bonneville-Aptot were shocked when Honora announced that she was leaving Grand-père's house at the farm to move in with her new boyfriend in Deauville. Eric reminded himself that Honora was a hard, determined, and creative manager. With zero experience in the restaurant business, she had taken Eric's Restaurant de la Tour from relative obscurity to one of the most popular attractions for miles around, making *beaucoup d'argent* even in the off-season.

"Quelle belle surprise, Honora ma chérie! Tout va bien en Normandie?" It was early Monday morning, and Chantal Favre was touched that her darling girl was calling. It was a lovely invitation to lunch at the Ritz Hotel in the lovely Conservatory dining room. She knew Jacques was free the following Saturday and immediately accepted Honora's invitation. The wise litigator had already guessed the reason for Honora coming to Paris to take her parents to lunch. It must be to meet this boy, Philippe, who she is seeing. Wonderful that there is finally a man in her life. I hope he is a good young man from a good family.

Following Philippe's dramatic revelations the night before when he stopped at Pont Auzhou, Honora had confided to Grand-père Riaux that she, most likely, would be moving to Deauville to live in Philippe's condo on the water. She dearly loved her grandfather. He had been her refuge and her strongest ally after she escaped from her difficult situation in Paris.

"Of course, I suspected that you soon would leave me, my *poupée*. I have heard very good things about your young man. His cousin, the Comtesse d'Osmoy, thinks the world of him, and so do others in the region that have known him since he was small. He is to be admired. For a child to grow up in a home like his—with so much misery and instability—is a terrible, sad thing. Apparently, he turned out to be the opposite of his father, the Duc d'Orléans."

Honora took all of this in and slowly digested it. It sounded ominous, but she was too happy and excited to worry about what her grandfather was saying. She wrapped her arms tenderly around his shoulders and smacked a loud kiss on top of his shiny, bald head. He was seated at the head of the kitchen table, a simple piece of wood furniture that had witnessed countless triumphs, discussions, and dilemmas over many years. She never doubted that old Maurice would understand how she felt about Philippe and that it was time for her to take the next step in growing up.

As she walked out of the house, Honora completely forgot Grand-père's remarks about Philippe's family. She would find out soon enough.

The Mini Cooper was washed, waxed, and carefully vacuumed for the drive to Paris that Saturday. Philippe was concerned about the ingoing traffic to Paris and some road closures. He picked up Honora at Grand-père's exactly at 9 a.m. This was the first time Honora had ever seen him in a formal, white cotton shirt, gold cuff links, silk tie from Charvet on la rue de la Paix, and of course, a navy gabardine blazer over gray slacks. *Papa will be impressed that Philippe shops at Charvet.*

Honora had a good feeling about introducing Philippe to her parents. It was also a meeting of reconciliation, or at least she hoped that it would be. She picked the Ritz Conservatory restaurant for its elegance and formality. It was an old-world place of impeccable manners, civilized behavior, and restraint. In whatever way Chantal and Jacques reacted to their daughter's news, it would be impossible to make a scene there or say anything rude or negative. She was safe at the Ritz.

The Place Vendôme, where the Ritz Hotel was ensconced, was glorious that Saturday. The 145-foot-high bronze Vendôme Column was the centerpiece of the enormous square. It had recently been restored by the Al-Fayed Charitable Foundation. Al-Fayed was a fabulously successful Egyptian businessman, buying and recreating the great Harrod's department store in London and the Paris Ritz Hotel. Most people identified him as the father of Dodi Fayed, who tragically perished in 1997 with Diana, princess of Wales, in a car accident minutes after they left the Hotel.

The sinister dead Corsican still followed Honora around even that day, as she and her Philippe were arriving in Place Vendôme. In 1803 Napoleon decided that France must have something similar, but better, than Trajan's 126 foot high Roman column to commemorate his fast-growing military power all over the world. The arrogant Corsican insisted to the designers of his own "Austerlitz Column" that his statute must stand at the top of the creation. As Philippe and Honora swung around the Place Vendôme, Napoleon seemed to look down at them from his column in the center of the square. The day was warming up to the seventies and the sun was shining. The traffic and pedestrian tourists filled the square, looking at the shop windows and stopping to gaze at the palatial entry, covered in thick, royal-blue carpet, to the Ritz Hotel.

Philippe was a great driver. Growing up in Paris, he navigated the city's heavy traffic easily. Ahead of schedule, he eased the Mini in front of the Ritz valet. Philippe took Honora's hand as she got out of the car and held it tightly while they entered the hotel and walked down the long, carpeted hallway to the restaurant. Chantal and Jacques were at the table and rose to kiss their returning triumphant girl. *"Maman, Papa je vous présente Philippe."*

It was smooth sailing all the way for the lovers. The Favres, obviously, knew in advance all about Ferdinand Philippe Thouroude d'Orléans. They knew more about his background than Honora. Philippe was the son and heir to one of the nine dukes of France and a blood relation to the Bourbon royal line of

French and Spanish kings. They were blown away that their daughter somehow had made this royal catch not in Paris society but instead in a Normandy farmers' village. The couple discussed their daughter's situation and tried to figure out why Honora would go to so much trouble to return to Paris with her boyfriend.

"Jacques, please try to be patient with her and listen to what she is coming to say. Think about everything that Honora has accomplished since she left us. Now she has met a young man, apparently with impeccable education and pedigree." Chantal was not apprehensive about seeing her daughter again; Grand-père called her often with updates on Honora—all positive.

After everyone ordered an apéritif, Jacques Favre asked Honora if she remembered Khaled, the long- time office supply delivery man at the law firm. Her curiosity piqued at such a question because she had recently sighted Khaled talking to a man on a scooter while shopping with Philippe at the Sunday Deauville farmers' market. Khaled appeared to have handed a black sports bag to the man, who quickly drove away.

Philippe recognized Khaled at the market. He had seen him before at the fishing boats at Barneville-Cateret. Odd that this Khaled was acquainted with Youssef, the delivery man he was filling in for last August. Philippe remembered that the two spoke only for seconds as the boats unloaded as if exchanging quick messages before they took off in opposite directions. It was Philippe's final day on the job, and he was in a hurry to collect his pay and leave.

Neither Honora nor Philippe thought any more about it—a coincidence, they assumed. Until Jacques Favre told them that an INTERPOL detective named Yasmine Lagarde visited the cabinet that past week to question Christine Paul. Her cell number was on Khaled's personal mobile contacts, according to police who searched his personal belongings for clues. The detective revealed that Khaled died in a mysterious late-night truck crash on the A13 a few days before. The truck went off a high bridge crossing on the A13 motorway just after the Deauville exit.

The inspectors on the scene discovered that the truck's brake cables were cut. They found at least ten million euros worth of contraband opiates and crack cocaine inside; hours later, after checking video footage from traffic cameras, the vehicle was traced to a vessel docked at Barneville-Cateret. The ship's manifest showed it departed Mumbai and entered the Mediterranean Sea at the Suez Canal. The ship's captain had gone missing by the time INTERPOL finally searched the vessel, and the Sri Lankan registry papers found on board could not be verified.

Jacques Favre didn't concern himself too much with the detective's visit. After all, Madame Paul directly ordered everything from Khaled for the office. It was perfectly normal that her number would be in his contacts, his instincts told him. Favre's bullish personal opinions were tripping him up. Again.

CHAPTER 8

The Spanish Donkey

The Christmas lights with the mass of blue pine wreaths and swags and the blazing red poinsettias, amaryllis, and cyclamens blanketed the Deauville town center. The clamors against wasteful power consumption from local Green Party leaders fell on deaf ears. Deauville's town council voted overwhelmingly in favor of keeping the public holiday decorations illuminated every night from the first of December until after New Year's 2020. It attracted greater numbers of holiday shoppers, they said.

The young couple was settled in the condo near the Yacht Club. After Honora moved in, the tiny apartment felt pretty cramped. But they loved the view of the yachts anchored in the private marina below their balcony and the sound of the seagulls. As planned, Honora kept her restaurant job in Le Bec, but because of the long drive in the dark after the dinner service, her hours were scaled back. She had purchased her cousin Bruno's 2005 Land Rover. Her first ever car buy. She didn't mind the rust inside because it had low mileage and relatively new tires. The faded green exterior retained its classic look, and Honora thought it coordinated with her green eyes. It was good, basic transportation, and it was cheap. Honora was learning the value of money.

By now, she was accustomed to the drive from Deauville to Le Bec and arrived early as usual, worked the lunch service, and supervised the dinner set up. Véronique LeNormand was back at the restaurant, this time as a salaried employee. She took over the management duties for the dinner service, clean-up, and closing. After Véronique graduated from the public lycée in Bourg Achard, Eric hired her full-time. People like her didn't worry about le Bac; getting a local job as soon as possible was their priority.

Despite her busy work schedule and helping at home, Véronique had blossomed into a size XXL Viking girl. Chef Luc began calling her la Big Red, and Honora and the two new busboys did the same when she could not hear them. The nickname was more a gesture of affection than ridicule. Actually, Luc had become quite fond of la Big Red, particularly when she demonstrated that she could also be la Big Marketing Genius. Eric had been worried about a downturn in the restaurant reservations during the winter months and shared this with the staff.

Véronique came up with a clever idea to attract customers for holiday office lunches and the like. Using her Samsung phone, she began taking short videos of the chef preparing his dish of the week. The weekly videos were posted on the restaurant's Facebook page and Instagram. The videos went viral; thousands of viewers raved about the new dishes every week, and the restaurant was booming with business. After the second video, the online reservations shot through the roof—fully booked through January 2020. Eric was impressed, and the Pavarotti in the kitchen was ecstatic. La Big Red made Chef Luc into an instant culinary celebrity on the internet. The temper tantrums in the kitchen became few and far between.

Vinci promoted Philippe to assistant foreman at the Barbot Hotel construction site. He earned it with his long work hours and ability to take over and solve logistical problems on the spot. What was strange to Honora was that he rarely mentioned his parents; work talk was Philippe's main topic of conversation. She wasn't sure if Philippe had ever told his parents about her or their living arrangements in Deauville. Once in a while, she would see a call notification from his mother, Isabelle Amelia.

He will tell me when he's ready. I don't need to pry into his family affairs. Anyway, the only thing that matters is that Philippe loves me. Honora reassured herself that there was nothing wrong with Philippe's evasiveness about his parents. What still bothered her were the remarks about Philippe's father that Grand-père made to her weeks ago. She had not been able to completely forget.

Honora's bank account balance at Société Générale was the highest in her life; one day, she received a complimentary Visa credit card in the mail. She was an upwardly mobile businesswoman; her net worth steadily increased because she saved most of her earnings. Philippe refused to let Honora share the condo's expenses, and her hectic work hours left little time for shopping. But she had plans.

I'm going to save my first charge on the Visa for Philippe's Christmas gift. He's going to love it. Honora had been looking at men's wallets in the Louis Vuitton Boutique in Deauville. After going back to the boutique a couple of times, she decided on a black leather wallet with the LV embossed in the same color on the lower-right corner of the wallet. It was elegant yet discreet; the textured, treated leather on the exterior sides wreaked Vuitton style but in an understated way.

As she took out her new Visa card to pay, she asked the sales attendant to arrange for Philippe's initials to be hot stamped in silver letters on the inside flap. The attendant was impressed as he filled out the order: FPTO. He knew aristos had four initials, not two or three like ordinary people.

She found some small items for Grand-père, as well as for Maman and Papa around the corner at Aigle, but she decided to wait closer to Christmas before making those purchases. Honora wanted to confirm their holiday plans with her parents. Since their lunch at the Ritz, she had not heard anything from Maman and wondered if something was wrong at home or at work.

It was a Monday night after she had made the Louis Vuitton purchase. December had arrived with cold, frigid winds, even along the Deauville coastline, which was somewhat protected from the North Sea gusts. Being her day off, she had strolled from the Vuitton boutique to the Place de Morny circle to her favorite delicatessen, Breton Traiteur.

It was the only place that prepared fresh salmon tart twice a day— morning and afternoon. It was Philippe's favorite for a light, weekday dinner followed by fromage Pont l'Évêque. Because the old establishment received daily shipments from the dairies just outside the town center, all cheese sold at Breton's was unpasteurized. It was the richest, most flavorful, and most nutritious cheese imaginable and, of course, could not be transported long distances nor exported to foreign lands. The gastronomic delight was consumed exclusively by Deauville's privileged locals.

Philippe walked through the door at 7:30 p.m., as usual. Without saying a word, he walked behind Honora, put his arms tightly around her waist, and covered the nape of her neck with warm, slow kisses. She was facing the kitchen counter, slicing the fresh salmon tart and serving the slices on their dinner plates. She could feel his body getting warm and aroused while he pressed against her derrière. The only thing Honora could think of was to grab a piece of tart, whip around to face him, and stick it in his mouth. Then she kissed him hard while he was trying to chew the tart. Their dinner got cold while the young lovers pulled each other into the bedroom.

Philippe penetrated her tenderly and profoundly, as if he was taking refuge in Honora's body, running away from someone or something. His thrusting was slow and deliberate—not a savage act like their sex before. Philippe wanted this moment to last forever; he was holding back his climax. Honora felt her orgasm prolonged like never before. This time their lovemaking reached a higher, almost metaphysical plane. His release finally came with full force.

She felt him relax and collapse inside her vagina; he stayed there for a few seconds. She waited for him and couldn't figure out what he was doing different. He's taking longer to come out and doing something different with his condom. Then she felt him pull out and quickly walk into the bathroom to finish removing the torn condom and wash.

Philippe said nothing to her about the torn condom when he finally returned to their bed. He just hugged Honora as tightly as he could. Honora could feel something was not right, but she just went with the moment. They cuddled on the crumpled blue sheets. She loved to stroke the wiry, dark hair on his chest— touching Philippe was soothing to Honora.

She thought Philippe had fallen asleep with her caresses, but it turned out he was organizing his thoughts. Then he whispered, "For Christmas Day lunch, we are going to see my parents in Paris. I hope you are not too disappointed, my darling. However the visit turns out, I love you, and that is the only thing that matters." His voice had some regret or sadness in it.

There was not enough space for a Christmas tree or a nativity display in their tiny condo. Still, Honora hung hundreds of mini Christmas lights in multiple swags on their balcony overlooking the marina. She hid

Philippe's gift at the restaurant, waiting until Christmas Eve when they agreed to exchange gifts. He tried to be coy about her gift, but Honora could sense something big was in the works. She knew that Philippe was receiving emails from someone at the Cartier flagship store on rue de la Paix. For the last few days, she had glanced at the notifications on his cell phone screen while they were having breakfast.

It was her regular Monday off at the restaurant, the beginning of Christmas week 2019. Deauville teemed with last minute shoppers, many coming from as far as Paris to see the display of holiday lights and the thirty-foot-high spouting fountain at the Place de Morny. Honora was checking her emails and catching up on calls. She saw a text from Papa. Call me or your mother as soon as you read this. Honora was not accustomed to receiving curt commands from her father via text. Strange.

Is somebody ill? she thought. She felt uneasy when she dialed Papa's cell; it was 10 a.m., and Jacques Favre most likely would not answer if he were in a hearing. She was getting ready to leave a voicemail when he picked up.

"*Allô, chérie, comment vas-tu? Comment va Philippe? Maman et moi vont très bien. Je suis à la cour maintenant, très occupé, mais je voulais te dire que la détective d'INTERPOL, Madame Lagarde, vien te voir à Deauville. Christine Paul a été assassinée, son corps à été retrouvé par la police dans la Seine, hier matin.*"

It was like a bomb detonated in her head. Surely there had to be some mistake. Maybe the dead woman floating in the Seine wasn't Madame Paul, after all? And why was this INTERPOL agent coming to see her in Deauville?

A flood of questions and suppositions filled her mind. She felt sad, of course. Her old boss was a mean, heartless bitch, but she didn't deserve to be murdered if it was true. Honora immediately tried to call Philippe at work. Philippe didn't pick up, but he rarely did while at work. She sent a brief text: Madame Paul dead. Cops coming to apartment.

Shortly after noon, she saw a text from Detective Lagarde: Outside your building. Have some questions. Assume you know.

Honora tried to steady her right hand. It shook as she poured a glass of Mont Blanc water for the detective. Philippe had not replied to her call or text; Honora was beginning to worry about being alone with a cop.

Yasmine Lagarde was short with dark skin. Being a higher-up at INTERPOL, she was not in uniform. But she was packing. Her shoulder harness peeked out from underneath her gray, wool blazer as she walked up the stairs to the apartment. She looked stylish yet professional, wearing black, opaque tights with two-inch heel leather pumps. Her black, straight hair and piercing, dark eyes no doubt came from her Moroccan mother.

But her mental cunning and determination came from her French-born father, a career gendarme who died in a shoot-out with narcotics traffickers. Yasmine loved her job; it was her entire reason for living. She was single, never married and never planned to be. She had no friends nor social acquaintances. Her only relationships were with her coworkers on the force. They rarely saw her smile or laugh. And Detective Yasmin hated the diabolical network that operated a multi-billion-euro drug trade throughout Europe.

She got down to business after taking a small sip of the Mont Blanc. "When was the last time that you had contact with Christine Paul, and what was the purpose of that contact? Do you know anyone who had recent contact with her other than those working in your father's cabinet? Are you acquainted with a man named Khaled who made office supply deliveries to your father's law firm when you worked there? Are you acquainted with a man named Youssef?"

Honora replied calmly and carefully to the detective's questions. She had nothing to hide, after all. The interrogation didn't last more than twenty minutes. Honora was relieved. Yasmine Lagarde was quite taken with Honora's candor and honesty about her difficult relationship with la Paul. The seasoned INTERPOL operative divulged more than was appropriate during an interrogation. As their exchange concluded, Lagarde sensed Honora was clean and didn't have details relevant to the investigation.

Honora was faced with a reality so evil it was like stepping inside a Stephen King horror book. After her interrogation was over, Lagarde let her guard down and talked openly to Honora. Because of the particularly grotesque state of the corpse when retrieved from the water, France's top forensic examiner was flown in from

Marseille to conduct the autopsy. His team determined that Christine Paul had been brutally murdered riding a "Spanish donkey," a medieval torture device made of wood and iron spikes shaped like a wooden horse. It was used exclusively on women.

Naked women were seated on the horse and began to bleed from their genitals. After hours of sitting on the donkey, with weights hung from their feet, it cut their bodies in half. During the Spanish Inquisition in the fifteenth century, women accused of heresy were interrogated and murdered in this horrific manner. In recent months, undercover INTERPOL reported that the Russian mafia used it to eliminate insiders who broke the rules. It sent a chilling message.

What did la Paul do to perish in this unspeakable manner? Was she doing something illegal with Khaled, after all? Was she mixed up with Youssef? Honora probably would never know the answers to her questions. She couldn't wait to share the shocking news with Philippe.

It was 7 a.m. Tuesday—Christmas Eve—and Honora hadn't slept all night. Her many calls, text messages, and even emails to Philippe the day before and all through the night were not answered. Philippe had never done this before. Panic began to set in.

Thankfully, the restaurant only offered a lunch service on the twenty-fourth; the two lunch sittings began at 11 a.m. for two hours each. Honora and Véronique waited on a full house with the two busboys and Chef Luc. The special price gourmand Christmas menu that Luc had designed was unprecedented, phenomenal; Eric expected them to gross a week's receipts in that single day.

Honora was a trooper; she couldn't possibly let the restaurant down regardless of her turmoil. She shared the Find My iPhone app with Philippe in case anything ever happened to either one of them. So far, she had been unable to register a location for Philippe's phone on her app. His phone was off, or the location service was deactivated. She worked through Christmas Eve at Le Bec in a fog of worry and dread. Véronique could tell something was off with Honora; she mercifully offered to supervise the clean-up and closing. Honora took off at 3 p.m.

Grand-père was Honora's rock: wise adviser, supporter, and mentor. From le Bec, she drove the oil-burning Land Rover directly to the farm outside Bonneville-Aptot. He was outside changing a gargantuan rubber tire on one of the tractors when Honora pulled up. Maurice's *poupée* jumped out of her vehicle and ran into his arms. His overalls were covered with black grease from removing the flat tire, but she didn't notice. Honora howled like a wounded animal when Maurice asked, *"Qu'est-ce qui se passe, poupée?"* He wanted to know what had happened to his little one that caused her such torment. He carried Honora's full weight into the kitchen to sit down. She had collapsed in his arms out in the tractor yard.

"There is only one way to find out what happened to your young man. We must go to Chateau d'Aptot at once and speak to the Comtesse. She is his mother's cousin and is bound to know something."

It was only a little past 4 p.m., but it was already dark when they reached Aptot. Maurice had called for an immediate audience and apologized to the Comtesse for being so rude. It was a family emergency, he said. The grand portail opened for them as soon as they reached the entrance to the alleé. The long driveway was lined with five-story-high tilleul trees, which looked like ancient skeletons; their final leaves of 2019 had dropped weeks before.

Little had changed in the grand salon of Château d'Aptot since the last time Maurice was there. It was the size of a ballroom and had a fireplace so big that it could roast up to five upright humans at a time. The wood fire crackled and spat out big sparks, which landed on the cast-iron screen.

He and Honora were ushered to the twelve-foot-long table in the salon; they sat on the upholstered chairs of gold silk brocade. Maurice was relieved that before leaving the farm, he discarded the greased, black overalls for some clean khakis and the pristine, blue oxford shirt that he saved for Sunday Mass. Honora still wore faint grease stains on her blouse, but their hostess didn't seem to notice.

The Comtesse looked at Honora with pity and concern; she steeled herself to speak. "Philippe is going through a very hard time right now. His father, the Duc d'Orléans, is dead. The police insist on an autopsy, but it is suspected that he took his own life sometime yesterday afternoon. My cousin, Isabelle, has authorized me to pass this very private information on to you. She is in deep mourning for the death of her husband and is extremely worried about how this terrible tragedy will affect her son. Philippe was with her in Paris late yesterday, hours after she found her husband's body in his study. My advice is to be patient and give Philippe some time to mourn his father. I have known this boy all his life and assure you that his relationship with the Duc was not a happy one. Tragically, the Duc lived a dissipated and decadent life and could not be a good father to Philippe. Wait for Philippe to make peace with his father's memory and get his head straight. He is a good and honorable man, and I expect that he will contact you when he is ready."

Grand-père clutched Honora's hand in his own the entire time the Comtesse was speaking. It was like when he held the tiny hand of the toddler walking through his orchards on those hot August days. He was protecting her, as he had all her life. Honora steadied herself, leaning against Grand-père as they stood up from the table. *"Comtesse je vous remercie infiniment. Je prendrai vos conseils à cœur et me souviendrai toujours de votre gentillesse en ce moment difficile.* I beg you to keep me informed should you have any further news about Philippe. He is my life. My whole life." Honora was eternally grateful for the kindness shown by the Comtesse; the words and advice she had heard that evening were tucked deep inside her heart and would not be forgotten.

CHAPTER 9

Mont-Saint-Michel

Never in her worst nightmares had Honora ever experienced sad, dark, hopeless days like these. Since Philippe had vanished on Christmas Eve, she had tried to hold on and go about her normal life. At least superficially. The restaurant business was a godsend during Christmas and New Year's week.

It kept her so occupied and stressed with her management duties that the weeks went by quickly. By the last days of January 2020, she could no longer bury the agony she felt. Not one single word or message, direct or indirect, from Philippe. Intentionally, she had not updated her parents about her situation, although Honora knew Grand-père was in regular contact with her mother. Honora kept hoping that Philippe would return at any moment, and her life would return to normal.

The only clue that Philippe was still of this world was something the live-in apartment manager, Benoit, told Honora shortly after New Year's Day. Honora was worried about the monthly rent for the apartment. She was prepared to pay the January rent, which she assumed was due. Early one morning as she locked the apartment to drive to Le Bec, she saw Benoit downstairs and asked about payment instructions for the apartment rent. Benoit was in his early twenties and grateful for the nice lodging and modest salary he received as an apartment manager.

His accent and simple vocabulary and idioms were from the remote part of Brittany, a rural, rocky land surrounded by the sea where most inhabitants scarcely earned a living from fishing, cultivating a few apple trees, or raising dairy cows. It was back-breaking work, and Brittany country people had a short longevity. He was a man of few words, probably because of his lack of formal education, but Benoit was handy with repairs and always willing to help the tenants.

He asked her to follow him into his cubbyhole office to check his computer records on rents. *"C'est déjà réglé, Mademoiselle.* The rent payments are paid by automatic debit from an account at Banque Paribas Paris." Those simple words from Benoit sounded heavenly. *Surely the monthly debits on the account would have stopped if Philippe were dead. But where is he? Why has he quit on me like this?* The thoughts rang out like church bells inside her head. The information from Benoit cut through Honora like a sharp saber. It also lit a tiny flicker of hope.

On her next day off from the restaurant, she decided to drive to the Paris Apple Store behind the place de l'Opéra. She was going to plead with the Genius Bar gurus to get a location signal on Philippe's iPhone. Her phone had location sharing with Philippe's, and she felt she had a right to the information. Something odd happened at the Genius Bar. "*Désolée, mademoiselle, mais cet appareil a été désactivé depuis le 23 décembre. Nôtre politique de confidentialité signifie que je ne peux pas vous en dire plus.*"

Honora was suspicious when the tech gave her mixed messages. Initially, the Apple tech was very friendly and assured her that they could help with the location. She handed him her iPhone, and he took it somewhere in the store via the employee elevator. He was gone with her device for nearly a half-hour. When he returned to the Genius Bar, his expression was different—more businesslike and detached. He was sorry, but Philippe's iPhone had been deactivated since December 23. Company protocol prohibited him from revealing more details. One more dead end.

A wasted day and a wasted five hours of driving. At least I can swing by the cabinet to tell my parents what is happening; that is, if either one is at the office now. Maman must be so worried; I have not returned her calls or texts recently. I will surprise her. Honora's mind was multi-tasking in thoughts and ideas, searching for solutions to find the only man she had ever loved.

In a quick reflexive reaction, she swung the Land Rover into an empty meter space in front of the entrance to 15 avenue de l'Iéna. It was the same space reserved for Khaled's delivery van, she remembered.

"Chérie, quelle charmante surprise! Je suis très heureuse de te voir!" Chantal Favre was surprised and happy to see her daughter and hugged her lovingly. She put her arm around her daughter's waist and led her from the big reception hall to the formal, glass- enclosed conference room.

Like all the renovated rooms in the cabinet, the conference room was spacious and utilitarian and filled with natural light. The white, rectangular plexiglass table in the center of the room was covered in neatly stacked court pleadings, exhibits, and thick folders. The coordinating fifteen Roche-Bobois charcoal-black swivel chairs were arranged against the glass walls to make room for all the work going on around the table.

La Maître Favre was preparing her ammunition for a tough trial. She noticed that Honora had transformed from when she lived at home on the rue de Constantine. Life and love had made her noticeably thinner, and she behaved a little more on edge, nervous. Her green, cat-like eyes had crow's feet, and her face was gaunt. Philippe's mysterious disappearance had taken its toll.

This was their first face-to-face meeting since the happy lunch with Philippe at the Ritz last year. Chantal was touched by her daughter's impromptu visit. She had been waiting for the right occasion to confide many things to Honora, and now that Jacques was away in court, it was a good time to have this womanly, heart-to-heart talk. What Chantal needed to say to Honora had to be divulged only in person and in private.

First, her hand-written condolence note to Philippe's mother, Isabelle Amelia, Duchesse d'Orléans, had been received, and a simple, pre-printed card of appreciation was sent back in reply. Chantal had written her cell number below her signature on the note, hoping for a phone call from the grieving widow. Nothing. Clearly, the Duchesse had no intention of communicating with the Favres about her son.

Second, through the law firm's vast network of lawyers, judges, and law enforcement contacts, Chantal and Jacques obtained information on Philippe's family background and what might have triggered his unexplained, prolonged absence. Surely, it was not just because he was grieving for his father. She hoped that what she was about to say would provide some relief or comfort to Honora.

Chantal asked the receptionist not to disturb them in the conference room until further notice, and then she silenced her cell phone. The Duc d'Orléans, Philippe's father, was a reprobate, a twisted man. Despite the love and patience of his wife, Isabelle Amelia, Duchesse d'Orléans, née Theroude, and many years of psychiatric therapy, he had a proclivity for young male prostitutes and for beating and mutilating them after engaging in sex. He roamed the streets of Pigalle after midnight on weekends, "shopping" for the right victim.

Some of his victims were permanently injured, and some were even brutally and permanently disfigured. Over decades of bribing police to dismiss criminal charges and paying exorbitant amounts to settle private lawsuits resulting from the duke's vices, the d'Orleans family fortune became severely depleted. That is why Philippe dedicated himself to his studies and to building a successful career.

Honora was sobbing as her mother continued to speak slowly, deliberately, and kindly. Philippe's father was found in the family apartment by his wife, the Duchesse. The autopsy, which was done by order of the Paris prefecture of police, confirmed that it was suicide by self-inflicted gashes to his carotid artery. Death occurred in seconds.

The duke had been despondent for weeks before his death, most likely because he faced criminal charges for possessing illegal objects. His prized, secret collection of World War II German memorabilia had been discovered and confiscated by the police prefecture. He had been collecting Nazi memorabilia for many years and had spent more than ten million euros amassing his collection. The Duchesse cooperated with the police inspector, who executed the confiscation order, and told the inspector that her husband was particularly fond of Nazi SS weapons, uniforms, caps, and accessories.

"My darling girl, your father and I have been extremely distraught over what happened to you with Philippe. We do not blame the boy for running away, and we hope that he has not met the same demise as his father. We pray that Philippe will come to terms with his family history and return to you someday. But you cannot be sure of that or live your life waiting for him."

Honora and her mother were seated side by side on chairs facing the outside wall of the conference room—which was a twelve-foot-high, floor-to-ceiling window. Only the high backs of the chairs were visible to anyone outside the conference room who might happen to pass in the hallway. When Chantal finished speaking, she turned her chair to face her daughter. They both fell into each other's arms and cried. They cried for the loss of Honora's fairytale future with Philippe. It was unimaginable that their relationship would survive.

It was nearly 3 p.m. when Honora said goodbye to her mother. She was thinking about the Paris rush hour. It was Monday, and the onslaught of commuters leaving the city would begin very soon. She was emotionally exhausted and drained by the visit with Chantal and was in no condition to immediately drive back to Deauville. She was a wreck. Sitting in her rusty Land Rover in Khaled's old parking spot, she called Sandrine.

"Honora! I was just thinking about you in Normandy! Haven't been back in Paris very long. I was near you over the holidays but was crazy busy. My new choir gave two spectacular concerts for Christmas Mass and New Year's Day at Mont-Saint- Michel— more than one thousand tickets! Naturally, the hotels on the big rock were fully booked, and my singers had to take a hired bus back to their hotel in Avranches every night. Thankfully, our family apartment had not been rented out. I stayed there during the rehearsals and concerts. I am so sorry that we can't meet now. I'm swamped with work!"

After the break-up with Richard, Sandrine was extremely depressed for weeks. Somehow, her passion for classical music and her extraordinary talent for composition became a lifeline for Sandrine. She immersed herself in her music composition studies and assignments at the Sorbonne, and gradually, she recaptured her natural exuberance and *joie de vivre*— joy for life.

As a graduation project for her degree in classical music composition from the Sorbonne Conservatory, she founded a choir of classical, professional singers, Ensemble Parisii, named after the original settlers of the city of Paris. It was on fire. Concert invitations from all over France and even Italy were coming into their website.

Sandrine had never been so busy and successful in her life. She loved her darling friend, Honora, and so did not want to tell her that her final GPA was the highest ever in the history of the Sorbonne. She held the record for the highest grades ever at that great conservatory. *Honora is going through a tough time; I don't want to remind her of any school stuff or what happened to her here. We'll celebrate my grades later.*

Honora was thrilled and proud of her dear girlfriend and confidante. Since lycée, they both had gone through so much together. Now they both knew what it was to have your heart broken, your dreams of love shattered, in an instant and with no warning.

It gave her a lift just to hear Sandrine's voice, and she planned to stay in touch. "Ahh. Great! Let's plan for next time—either in Normandy or Paris. I understand how busy you must be with the ensemble. You are marvelous, my dear one. Bisous."

After the call, she drove up to a Starbucks and got a café noir. She got on the *périphérique*, which looped around the city and was already building up traffic bottlenecks, and headed to the A13 motorway to Normandy. Honora kept to the speed limit, eighty miles per hour. She was not in a hurry to get back to a dark, empty apartment in Deauville. It had too many memories. Benoit's information about the monthly automatic withdrawals for rent kept flashing in her head. It was significant.

Honora slept less than four hours after returning to Philippe's apartment. It was no longer her "home" with the man of her life. Although their life together lasted only a matter of weeks—not months or even years—Honora could not imagine her future without Philippe. They had made so many wonderful plans. Lying in bed, she meditated and began to see a plan for tracking him down. Philippe loved telling Honora about his long, hectic days at work and his big plans for learning the construction business and, in good time, starting his own company. However, Honora never visited the Vinci construction site for the Barbot Hotel and Golf Resort where Philippe was working every day. She never had reason to go there. Until now.

Her morning Nespresso buzz emboldened her to visit the Vinci construction site. She decided to do it now before she lost her courage. She quickly showered, dressed for work, and took off. She planned to make a quick visit, speak to someone at Vinci, and then drive to the restaurant at Le Bec to prepare for the Tuesday lunch service. It was typically slow early in the week, so she could be a little late.

As her Land Rover rolled up to the summit of the Mont Canisy, overlooking the Deauville town center, Honora prayed for guidance, wisdom, and stamina to continue searching for Philippe. She prayed for God to steer her to the right person at Vinci. Somebody, anybody, who knew and cared about her man.

At 7 a.m., Honora stopped her vehicle at the security gate of Vinci. The five-acre construction site was secured with three-meter-high, chain-link fencing, with surveillance cameras along the entire perimeter. There was only one access point. The guard asked for her name and searched the visitors' roster on his tablet. He looked up at Honora, shrugging his shoulders with a slight smile. She identified herself as Philippe's fiance. *"Je suis la fiancée de Philippe d'Orléans."*

With that said, the guard nodded to Honora, lifted the gate's security arm, and waved her through. "Le Capitaine is inside that big, white trailer. Over there." She didn't understand who that was or how she would recognize le Capitaine, but she drove to where the guard pointed. As she navigated the deep, thick mud and gravel, she couldn't stop herself from looking at every worker's face. Searching for her man as if there had been some huge mistake and he was really there after all.

Sebastian Musement was the senior project manager for the Barbot development at Mont Canisy, Deauville. He spent approximately twelve hours a day at the site, mostly outdoors inspecting and directing the work. He would soon qualify for retirement benefits in his country—age sixty-two. Vinci asked him to stay on a bit longer until the whole project was finished—estimated completion day June 2022. He was their best foreman, a combination of drill sergeant, mechanical genius, and circus ringmaster. A physically imposing man, he was comfortable carrying his 250 pounds on his six-foot, three-inch frame. He was more muscle than fat.

Vinci had completed its most challenging and profitable construction projects with Musement at the helm. The company trusted him, and more important, so did his construction team. The men and women on the team called him "le Capitaine."

Nobody remembered when or how he got that nickname, but it stuck. Even to his face, they addressed him as "Capitaine."

He happened to be inside the trailer trying to reboot his company tablet when Honora cracked open the door and shyly uttered, *"Bonjour. Je cherche Philippe d'Orléans, je suis Honora Favre."* Le Capitaine looked up from his Samsung tablet. His face was weathered and covered with lines and furrows from decades of work and worry. But the tired eyes looking up at Honora were full of sympathy or even pity for her. Although it remained unsaid, he didn't understand why Honora waited this long to come asking questions about Philippe. He was expected outside shortly; eight cement trucks were lined up, each rotating full mixers. The mammoth foundation was being poured that morning. While his big hand tried to smooth down his thick, overgrown crew cut, he reflected on what he would tell the beautiful, young Parisian standing in front of him.

"Ah. *Enchanté, Mademoiselle.*" Then, in a few seconds, he told her everything that company policy allowed him to reveal. Philippe had taken a temporary leave of absence from Vinci, but he was expected to return to this job. It was not known how long he would be away. However, Philippe was still in touch with certain team members who had taken over his duties. He was permitted to keep his company tablet to answer their questions.

Then le Capitaine called someone on his cell. It was the communications coordinator who kept track of all employee devices. "I have a daughter about your age, and I feel for you. But you must understand, I never told you what you are about to hear. The tablet Philippe is using showed a location in the vicinity of Mont-Saint-Michel. That was last week."

Honora nodded and thanked him as he was already trotting out the door to the cement trucks. She was so shaken that she had to keep a tight grip on the flimsy metal railing as she descended the trailer steps.

There was just enough time to drive to the apartment and throw some clean clothes and an extra pair of Nikes into one of her Longchamp totes. A few toiletries, her hairdryer, and her laptop and iPad fit into her backpack. She did not pack the Loestrin pills because she had stopped taking them until she had her next pap smear and general check-up. Since Christmas, her body was feeling different: dizzy spells and unexplained nosebleeds early in the morning. *Side effects from my contraceptives*, she thought.

Her uncle and boss, Eric Riaux, had replied to her text right away. His words were kind and sympathetic. "Yes. No problem taking off a few days from the restaurant. Véronique and Chef Luc have the two busboys to lend a hand." Honora also knew that since the holiday season, reservations were fewer and mostly on weekends. She wouldn't be missed.

Traffic moved at a normal pace when Honora reached the A13 motorway, direction northeast to Caen. She sped up to try to reach the Caen ring road before the crush of noon traffic. It could cut her travel time in half if she drove quickly around the town center to reach the A84 to Avranches. Once on the A84, it was less than one hour to reach the bay of la Manche straddling Normandy and Brittany and then cross to the island of Mont-Saint-Michel.

Only divine intervention, Honora believed, could have put her in contact with Sandrine the day before. That casual call to her friend while in Paris was not a coincidence. Sandrine replied in seconds to Honora's text that morning. Of course, she could use the de Rochefort family apartment at Saint-Michel. She would call the building concierge to expect Honora later that day.

Music is food for the soul. The radio in Honora's Land Rover was always on and tuned to her favorite radio station: FM 102.2 France Bleu Normandie. *It's a good omen,* she thought. Cheryl Crow was singing "All I Wanna Do" as she reached the outskirts of Caen. The fun and freedom and passion that she had known during the weeks with Philippe came flooding back as she listened to the lyrics. Sometimes, she would sing along with the radio while they drove in Philippe's Mini. It was her theme song, of sorts.

It's looking like I will get to the rock before 3 p.m., she told herself. Many Parisians referred to Mont-Saint- Michel as "the rock." The ring road around Caen was no problem, and she was now on the home stretch to Avranches the closest mainland town to her destination. At Avranches she would get off the motorway and drive cross-country to the sea and finally to the rock.

Honora was pleased with her driving and navigational skills. For a young, cosseted Parisian girl who grew up taking the Métro everywhere and had no car of her own until twenty-three, Honora had transformed herself into a seasoned driver in her new world—Normandy and now Brittany. Ten-lane motorways packed with fully loaded rigs coming from the cargo ships at Le Havre or single- lane dirt roads slicing through fields of crops or orchards were familiar territory to Honora. Wild and woolly Normandy had become her stomping ground.

Mont-Saint-Michel was a rock, literally. It was a tidal island off the coast of the common boundary between Normandy and Brittany. Originally part of the mainland of France, the colossal granite rock formed 525 million years ago out of red-hot, molten magma from beneath Earth's surface. Natural erosion over thousands of years separated the rock from the mainland and put it out in the sea about a half-mile away.

The Mont or mountain was more than 300 feet high, and it had a circumference of more than 3,100 feet. It looked like a gigantic *gâteau* or birthday cake rising to a tall peak or like a certain famous school of wizardry attended by a boy named Harry. Records show that people lived on the rock for hundreds of years before the birth of Christ; it was an important military stronghold for the Romans and much later for Hitler's German military. The deep quicksand visible at low tide lying between the island and the mainland deterred would-be invaders and marauders.

It was named after Michael the Archangel after he appeared to the Catholic bishop of Avranches in a vision in 708. Since then, its inhabitants believed that the Mont was protected by the Archangel and erected a statue of him that looked down from the roof of the abbey church at the highest point of the island.

What Philippe d'Orléans was doing at Mont-Saint-Michel was a mystery that Honora was determined to solve. Even if she found out the worst, it would give her some closure. She wanted to know, and then she could get on with her life.

The island came into plain view when Honora was about ten miles from the coast. She had seen it as a child, but not like this. It was covered by a blanket of stratocumulus clouds. Brilliant, white, puffy clouds seemed to spread out for miles across the top half of the island. The blanket of clouds hung so low over the rock that only the bottom half was visible from the mainland.

She parked her vehicle in the reserved parking lot next to the long bridge to the island. Only pedestrians were permitted on the Mont. A modern, electric-powered trolley took people across the bridge at all hours every day of the year—free of charge.

Because of the heavy cloud cover, darkness came early that evening at Mont-Saint-Michel—about four in the afternoon. Honora worried about unloading all her things from the Land Rover and hauling them to Sandrine's apartment in a single trip. It was impossible to know how far the apartment was on the rock and how far she would have to climb up the Grand Rue– the only street in the strange place. She was getting abominable cramps, and her lower back ached.

Honora finished stacking her belongings on the bluish-gray, crushed-gravel parking lot. Her taupe Longchamp tote was at the bottom of the stack, and it was getting wet, stained, and sticky with the gravel.

Lovely. What the hell will I do now? I can't possibly leave part of this here while I find Sandrine's apartment. Someone will pinch it before I return. Honora couldn't figure this out; she was tired and frustrated. She crouched down on the gravel, jamming as many items as possible into her backpack. It might work if she could load the backpack and drag the tote.

Suddenly, a pair of dusty cowboy boots were standing in front of her. Startled, she looked up. A big man wearing pressed, starched Levi's and a dark-brown Stetson cowboy hat was trying to speak to her. "Hi. Uhhh. I mean, boney joor. Can I help?"

Kevin Travis from Pflugerville, Texas, was terrific. An angel, actually. He was backpacking alone through Europe and had just arrived on a tour bus from Paris. Honora was delighted. "Oui! Thank you very much." Problem solved. Despite the language barrier, the attraction was mutual. She had never met an American before, and she definitely never expected to meet a cowboy from Texas.

After Kevin and Honora found the Rochefort apartment on the Mont, he helped her carry everything up the steep, narrow staircase of the building. It was so low that Kevin had to remove his Stetson to go up the stairs. The pied-à-terre was on the third floor. This was far from the grandiose residence on the rue de Constantine, but it was cozy and charming.

And the location was perfect. La Mère Poulard restaurant—world famous for its whipped omelets cooked over an open fire—happened to be steps away from the apartment. They made a dinner date for the following evening. As Kevin started to climb farther up the Grand Rue to find his hotel, he turned back to take one last look at Honora—obviously smitten.

He tipped his hat and said, "Ma'am, tomorrow is my treat, of course. Ya have a good night."

Honora had never heard this expression before, "my treat," but she was sure it meant something good.

As she unpacked her things in the apartment, Honora had an epiphany. She had not thought—at all—about Philippe while she was with the American.

CHAPTER 10

A Tall Texan

Why didn't she pack anything decent to wear? Honora felt really stupid for packing a mere jumble of long-sleeve sweaters, t-shirts, and jeans. Kevin would be waiting for her at La Mere Poulard's in exactly eight minutes. Thankfully, her hair was clean and styled with her trusty dryer, her nail polish and manicure were holding up, and her makeup was fresh and radiant. She was relieved to find one new pair of Ralph Lauren jeans thrown into the tote at the last minute.

When she pulled them up her slim legs and over her hips, the zipper wouldn't close all the way! A little paunch had appeared below her waist. Never mind. Honora flung her back on the bed, stretching her torso and sucking in her gut as much as possible, and finally zipped it. Then she realized that she was only half-dressed.

"I can't possibly wear a t-shirt or wrinkled sweater!" she told herself in panic. Time was running out. Desperate, she walked into the master bedroom and looked in the closet for anything that Sandrine might have left there. They both had the same taste in clothes. "C'est parfait! Anne Fontaine!" Three perfectly pressed, crisp, white cotton blouses were hanging there. "I'll get it laundered before I leave. I love the fluffy balloon sleeves!" Honora grabbed her backpack and ran out of the apartment. She was late, but no matter, she looked divine.

Kevin arrived well ahead of Honora and the 7 p.m. reservation time to watch the ritual of omelet preparation. He had just been seated when Honora appeared, flushed from the hectic dressing routine but alluring. Both were intrigued and impressed with what they saw around them. La Mere Poulard was a real person and a culinary legend. Her destiny took her from being a Parisian maid to creating a cooking style in the 1800s that became famous the world over.

The couple was seated at one of the choice tables in the big dining room; their table was barely twenty feet from the massive, wood-burning fireplace that was used for cooking Poulard's famous omelets. Dangerously close to the roaring fire inside the fireplace, young sous chefs, wrapped in starched, immaculately clean white aprons, were beating twenty eggs at a time in the biggest copper mixing bowl Honora had ever seen. A spectacular feat. After the eggs were so fluffy that they were spilling over the rim of the giant bowl, the mixture was poured into a twenty-inch cast-iron skillet and then quickly injected deep into the fire. The poised young chefs used skillets with five-foot-long iron handles, long enough for the skillets to reach deep into the hottest flames. The handles were coated with heat-resistant silicone. Outside, Asian tourists were ecstatic; they snapped away in a frenzy with their Nikons through the big window, amazed at the beauty and precision of the cooking.

Kevin Travis from Pflugerville was looking at another vision of beauty across the table. "Boo bell bow koo."

Honora did not laugh at his atrocious accent and silly attempt to tell her that she was very beautiful. Actually, she blushed and smiled. *"Merci. Parler en anglais, Kevin, je me débrouille."* Her years of English at the expensive Lycée Albert le Mun finally paid off. Honora told him to speak English; she could manage.

With that, Kevin launched into a heap of powerful talking and eating. For starters, they both decided to order the classic omelet prepared with unpasteurized butter, cream, and sea salt. After more than a century, the chefs still followed Annette Poulard's original dictum: cook only with the freshest local ingredients. Next, they asked for une grande bouteille de Mont Blanc, Honora's water of choice, and a cold Heineken for Kevin.

He took the first cold sip of his beer, and then he fixed his eyes on Honora and smiled before starting: "My name is Kevin Scott Travis. I grew up in a small town in Texas: Pflugerville. My father is the town doctor and still works there. My mom is the president of the town hospital." Honora couldn't take her eyes off her Texan for the next few hours except to cut pieces of her omelet. His green eyes twinkled the whole time he talked to her. He had smile lines on each side of his mouth, which deepened when he spoke. He was a ferocious eater and cleaned the big, oval platter in which his omelet was served and polished off two baskets of sliced baguettes.

Everything she saw and heard from Kevin impressed her. Kevin graduated December 2019 with a medical doctorate from the University of Texas–Galveston Medical School. He was accepted to the residency program in clinical virology at the Houston Methodist Research Institute. His residency was going to start in early May, and he would be staying with his aunt, who lived on North Boulevard, a prestigious address near the Houston Medical Center. The Medical Center was a sprawling compound of the world's most advanced hospitals, research facilities, and healthcare specialists employing more than 400,000 people. His paper on convalescent plasma therapeutics was published recently in the New England Journal of Medicine—the first student paper ever accepted for fast-track publication.

It was close to midnight when their waitress finally placed the check in front of Kevin. The restaurant was about to close, and they needed to clear their table, the last one occupied. Honora had known Kevin for little more than twenty-four hours, but she already knew more about him than she had ever known about Philippe, ostensibly the love of her life.

A thick sea mist came in from the bay and covered the rock while Kevin and Honora were having dinner, and the temperature plummeted. In the rush to dress and meet Kevin, she had run out of the apartment without her parka. Honora shivered as they walked outside; seconds later, she felt Kevin's arm wrap his warm jacket around her shoulders. It was only a few steps up the cobblestone street to Sandrine's apartment building; the walk back took only a few minutes.

But in that flash of time, Honora experienced something like never before. A sensation that someone was there to guard and protect her and be her champion, come what may. It was different than what she felt from Grand-pére, which was a grandfatherly love. With Kevin she felt stronger, like an energy field was all around her, and she was utterly cherished. They were just inside the door of the apartment building when she turned up her cold face to Kevin and said, *"Tu est mon ange guardien, Kevin. Merci pour tout."*

He cradled her face in the palms of his big hands and long fingers and gently kissed her forehead. Then he took both her hands and raised them to his lips. He kissed them warmly and lovingly, like he was paying homage to a queen. "Sleep well, Honora. I'll check on ya in da morn'n."

Philippe's Mini Cooper was in the parking lot on the mainland. Honora and Kevin had seen it one evening when they returned from having dinner in Avranches. It was definitely Philippe's car, and it had not been there very long. The hood was still warm. Honora's heart was racing as she looked inside the car. For something. Anything that might lead her to Philippe. That was the parking lot exclusively for visitors going to Mont-Saint-Michel. She had been there for several days. It was early February 2020, and the first moment that Honora knew, for certain, that le Capitaine's information about the IP address was accurate. Philippe was on the island. But where? And why? Honora had stopped calling and texting him days ago. All her attempts to find him were futile.

The day after they sighted the Mini, Kevin met Honora for breakfast at his hotel. She confided in Kevin about her morning dizzy spells and nosebleeds. The spells and bleeding were now lasting longer and coming nearly every morning—first thing. Honora was now more concerned, and she could not bring herself to call Maman or even her confidente, Sandrine. But she had Kevin, and he was a medical doctor.

Kevin was someone very special in her life. Although, they were not lovers. Not yet. Kevin could have taken her in their most private, passionate moments in the apartment. Honora would not have resisted. But he held back. It was the medical doctor in Kevin that would not cross the line with the beautiful French girl that he was beginning to fall in love with. Kevin listened quietly while Honora described the weeks of dizziness and bleeding from her nostrils.

He was not the Kevin that she knew at that point. His face was without expression yet deeply concentrated on her words. When she finished, he asked, almost in a whisper, "If you will allow me, I want to examine you. A routine physical examination will tell us more about what might be causing your symptoms." Then he reached for her right hand across the table and squeezed it reassuringly.

They walked to his hotel after breakfast to collect his instruments. He traveled with a small kit of basic medical tools in case of an emergency. Kevin suggested doing the exam in Honora's apartment; she would be more relaxed there. He was the son of a country doctor, and it showed in his caring, skill and concentration on his patient. It was a superficial exam, and Honora did not disrobe. It lasted about half an hour.

The last thing he did was return the stethoscope to her abdomen and listen. For the third time. Then, he gently hugged her and led her by the hand to sit at the tiny kitchen table and he sat in the chair next to her. "Honora, I did not detect any abnormality in the exam. However, because of your overt symptoms and what is coming through on my stethoscope, I advise you get a pregnancy test as soon as possible."

It was a Friday, and the closest pharmacy was in Avranches. It was not open on Saturday or Sunday. Suddenly, Kevin was not just a boyfriend anymore. He was her physician, her healer, her counselor. He could sense the panic beginning to take hold of Honora—that is when he decided to take control of the situation. He drove her Land Rover to Avranches and accompanied Honora to the pharmacy. They selected the ClearBlue Digital Pregnancy Test with the week indicator and immediately drove back to Honora's apartment on Mont-Saint-Michel.

Seven weeks. The test was positive, and the indicator showed a range of seven to ten weeks after gestation. The Loestrin pills never worked, and Honora conceived Philippe's child only days before he ran away. Kevin's arms held Honora while they sat on the bed and her body rocked back and forth, sobbing. She was back in the dark place. The place where she failed le Bac in 2015 for the second time after fear and panic set in to stop her from even opening the exam booklet.

"Hey. Listen here, Miss. You have me to lean on. Don't ya worry 'bout a thing. I don't have to be in Houston until late April, and I'll help you do whatever you decide." Kevin told her this as he kept his arms locked around her. Protecting her. Shielding her from her own sorrow. It was early Saturday morning when Kevin finally got up from the bed where he had held Honora all night. He quietly walked out of the apartment. An exhausted Honora was still asleep.

The call awakened Honora. *"Bonjour, Mademoiselle. C'est moi, Angelique.* I hope my call does not disturb you, but an ambulance came to your grandfather's farm this morning and took him. The EMT said it was a heart problem. Monsieur Maurice was taken to the Clinique de l'Europe in Rouen." There was a lot of worry in Angelique's voice.

Honora was still groggy and trying to process what Angelique said. *"Merci, merci beaucoup de m'avoir prévenu."* That was all Honora could manage: a thank you and very much appreciate your letting me know. It was close to noon on Saturday, and she wondered how long Kevin had stayed with her the night before.

She woke up to the fact that she was pregnant. Very pregnant. And that one of the most important people in her life, her grandfather, lay in a hospital in Rouen, victim of some heart episode, according to the housekeeper's call.

Honora instinctively made the call to her mother in Paris or wherever she was. Chantal spoke to her daughter for seconds only. She was speeding on the A13 motorway to Rouen. Early that morning, she and Jacques had been updated by the doctors on Grand-père's condition and prognosis. Possible bypass surgery, they said. He was the rock of the family, and Chantal had to be there for her beloved father.

Honora jumped into the shower, dressed, and then quickly walked up the road to Kevin's hotel. She was no longer back in the dark place. Her panic and fear about being pregnant had vanished. Overnight. She took long, steady strides, climbing uphill to the hotel, feeling buoyant.

My baby needs me now, and so does Grand-père. Chasing Philippe is a waste of my time and energy. Remember what the Comtesse d'Osmoy told me: He will contact me when he is ready. Anyhow, do I still love Philippe? Do I really need him? I have money and can work at many things now. Honora's thought process was working full throttle now, as she walked into the hotel lobby and texted Kevin. She had never felt so much in control of her destiny.

His reply text was instantaneous: "Be back in 10 minutes. Walking down from Abbey Mass." Honora stood outside of the Hotel le Mouton Blanc. It was cold. But the sun was out, and it warmed her. She remembered Kevin was a Catholic and was in the habit of attending weekly Mass on Saturdays or Sundays. When he saw Honora's text, Kevin was halfway down the multiple sections of stone steps leading down from the abbey church at the top of the island to his hotel.

In all, there were nine hundred steps to tackle coming down or going up to the abbey. It was not for the weak or faint-hearted. Mostly religious pilgrims and Catholic orders visited the abbey in the year 709 when it was dedicated to honor an apparition of Michael the Archangel. It was said that many of these supplicants climbed the steps on their knees to offer penance and mortification for their sins. Thousands of visitors climbed these steps every year to visit the abbey. For most of them, walking up the nine hundred steps was penance enough.

Dr. Travis was out of breath when he reached Honora outside his hotel. He was smiling but clearly preoccupied with something. He was carrying two shopping bags of books and souvenirs. They kissed on both cheeks and walked up the stairs to Kevin's room. When they went inside, Honora was surprised that his backpack and carry-on were packed and arranged at the door.

Kevin had a lot to say. "Methodist in Houston has expedited my residency start date to next week. Last night, I received an email from the chief of virology, my future boss. Some deadly contagion spreading through China is sounding off big alarms in the medical community. The entire Medical Center is preparing for the sickness to arrive in the United States in the coming weeks. They warned me that it is already in Europe. Apparently, it is a kind of highly contagious flu. I want to take you to your family before I leave. As soon as you are ready. You cannot stay here alone. Do you want me to drive you to Paris?" Kevin stroked her face and hair with both his hands and gently kissed her lips. He was her guardian angel, and Honora didn't hesitate to tell him all about what was happening to Maurice.

Kevin swung the Land Rover round into the circular valet entrance of the Clinique de l'Europe in Rouen; Honora jumped out and ran inside. Her heart ached for her dear grandfather. But she was there to comfort and help him and the family through this crisis. Honora was not a burden or victim any longer.

"Chérie, you are sweet to come so quickly to the bedside of Grand-père." Chantal kissed her daughter on both cheeks in the most warm and loving way when Honora hurried into the hospital room and then Jacques embraced her. Honora was relieved to see both her parents in the hospital room with Maurice. The old Normand was awake and lucid; oxygen tubes were inserted in his nostrils. His face lit up when he saw his granddaughter. Maurice's son, Eric, and his boy, Bruno, had arrived with the ambulance that morning, and they noticed the big change that came over Maurice when he saw Honora.

It was nearly 5 p.m. when she appeared. An hour before, both the clinician and the cardiac surgeon had done a second examination of Grand-père and given their recommendations to the family. A double coronary artery bypass was needed to restore normal circulation. Maybe a triple bypass would be done once the surgical team opened his chest and had a full view. Typically, a ten-to-fourteen-hour-long operation, the doctors predicted.

Answering a query raised by Jacques Favre about the mortality rate of such operations on a patient of eighty-eight years, the cardiac surgeon said, *"Environ dix pourcent."* Maurice's body was strong, and the doctors believed that his risk of death would only be about 10 percent, depending on postoperative complications. Her parents repeated what the doctors said to Honora. Word for word. She remained silent and stoic while taking it all in. They sensed something very different about her. Some kind of transformation in their girl.

Honora's father spoke first. "My dear, your mother and I are grateful that you are here. It is difficult and frightening to see Grand-père like this."

Then Maurice abruptly reached up to his face, with his arm still connected to an IV, and yanked off the oxygen tubes off. He cleared his throat. His voice was raspy from the medication, but he spoke with the same authority and force. "Take me home to my farm. There will be no surgery. No matter what. This is a small thing that happened. Maybe only a dizzy spell from not eating. Whatever it is, I'm going home."

Maurice's startling announcement was interrupted when everybody turned to see Kevin enter the hospital room. Chantal noticed that he was carrying his Stetson in hand and wearing cowboy boots. Kevin nodded a casual greeting to everyone in the room. He said, "Boney joor." With that, Chantal Favre understood perfectly that this was her daughter's "transformation."

Honora quickly stepped in to make the introductions. *"Maman, Papa, Grand-père, Oncle, j'aimerais vous présenter mon ami, le docteur Kevin Travis de Texas."* Then she explained how they happened to meet and become friends and that Dr. Travis was returning to the United States on an urgent assignment.

Kevin's appearance was disarming. During the short introduction, Maurice shot up in his hospital bed in a flash, quickly working the remote gadget to raise him to a sitting position. *"Medecin? Un Americain du Texas? Vous êtes très bienvenue, monsieur le docteur!* We haven't seen any of you round these parts since the War!" Maurice was highly animated and surprised to see the visitor. He nearly pulled out the needle in his IV as he outstretched his old, weathered paw to shake Kevin's hand.

Then, Jacques took a step closer to the young couple, curtly smiled, and held out his hand to welcome his daughter's new friend. Kevin returned Jacques's firm handshake. Eric and Bruno welcomed the American in the same manner: with a strong grip of the hand and a nod of the head. Neither of them had seen an American before, but they knew of such people from Maurice's stories about living through D-Day and the Liberation of France in 1944.

Chantal politely smiled and nodded her head. *"Enchanté docteur"* was all she could manage to say. This Honora was not the girl who left the family apartment on rue de Constantine. Chantal was in the presence of a different woman—self-assured, nurturing, loving, and comfortable in her skin. Maman suddenly understood what it was to have an empty nest—her little bird had flown away into the world.

CHAPTER 11

Fear and Forgiveness

She was back at the farm. At least for the time being. Since Kevin had captured the Favres' interest and trust at the bedside of old Maurice in the Rouen hospital, the world had changed dramatically before Honora's eyes. It was early March 2020. In the past weeks, everything was turned upside down.

Apparently, the entire planet was threatened with a deadly malady that nobody seemed to understand. Honora couldn't forget what Kevin told her about it that last day on Mont-Saint-Michel. It was catastrophic. Most that presumed to know the answers about what it was and how to treat it were opportunists maneuvering for power, fame, and fortune. The few medical experts with enough experience and integrity to identify the deadly virus were either ridiculed or shunned as charlatans. The all-powerful global media used a political filter to decide what should and should not be reported. In France, the general public's distrust of anything coming from their government only became more intense and entrenched. The fate of world powers shifted with the growing number of infections, as did the fate of millions of innocent human lives.

That February twilight, when the young Texas doctor walked into old Maurice's hospital room, had unleashed a flurry of decisions and disputes among the Favre and Riaux families and the doctors. Over the indignant protestations of Chantal and Jacques Favre—distinguished Parisian avocats à la Cour—and the attending cardiologists, the old Normandy farmer had discharged himself from the hospital the following day.

Eric and Bruno Riaux had never trusted doctors and sided with Grand-père. The documents releasing the hospital and his physicians of all further responsibility for his care were prepared by the hospital's legal department and then carefully explained and presented to the old Normand. He sat in the chair next to his hospital bed intended for visitors, and flourishing a Bic pen borrowed from his new friend, Dr. Travis, he carefully signed all the papers. *"Bon! C'est fait.* Now, get me the hell outta here." Honora and Kevin stood at his side and helped Grand-père out of the chair and out the door. He refused the customary wheelchair service for discharged patients, walking out on his own two feet and slowly climbing, sans assistance, into the front passenger seat of Honora's Land Rover.

Shortly after returning Grand-père to his home, Honora had driven Kevin to catch his departing flight. The lovers had said a quick *à bientôt* outside Terminal 2, Charles de Gaulle Airport. It was a "see you soon," not a "goodbye." They had every intention of seeing each other again soon.

Kevin did not want Honora to come inside. It would have been too hard to part surrounded by throngs of strangers. Her Land Rover was in the Deposé Minute parking slots with the motor running when he jumped out and took his luggage from the rear. Inside the vehicle, he had already kissed her forehead, cheeks, and lips while looking into her teary eyes.

He told her, "There is much to do now. For both of us. Me in Houston, and you here in France. This must be how couples in World War II felt, being torn apart. Know this, my love: I will return to you or send for you, with God's grace. We are meant to be together, you and I. And that includes the tiny person living inside you." Her eyes followed Kevin to the airport entrance, but he never looked back. Dr. Travis was already focused on saving lives at Methodist Houston.

It was perfectly natural and expected that Honora would return to her old manager job at the Restaurant de la Tour at Le Bec-Hellouin. The staff and the regular diners were happy to see her. Véronique had been the acting manager during Honora's absence. Part of her was relieved to see Honora back in charge. Chef Luc Carton was now an online celebrity chef. Thanks to Véronique's self-learned digital abilities, the restaurant's Facebook page had morphed into a popular national gourmet website with podcasts featuring the chef's new dishes offered at the tiny Le Bec restaurant.

Eric Riaux was over the moon; he had never imagined that the tiny restaurant in the middle of nowhere would be so successful. The only worry was the growing number of infections in France. Thousands were dying, and the hospitals were overrun with sick people. It was common knowledge that the sickness had started in China and spread quickly to the rest of the world, but global health organizations were afraid to blame anyone, especially the powerful Chinese Communist Party. They even hesitated to use the word pandemic, which, in fact, is exactly what it was. And the pandemic was killing more and more people every day. More and more people said that the deadly disease traveled silently and invisibly—through the air.

Honora was well past the first trimester of her pregnancy. But her long, lean figure barely showed it. She felt great, and the nosebleeds and dizzy spells had vanished. Grand-père was delighted when she moved back into the Riaux home at his farm. Her room was just as she left it when she moved in with Philippe the year before. So much had transpired since she left the farm at Bonneville. She wanted to keep busy, as busy as possible. Constant activity helped Honora keep her mind off the horrific shutdowns that were happening all over France. It also helped the time go by between emails, texts, and calls from Kevin.

He was pulled into a herculean effort at Houston Methodist Hospital and the Research Institute as soon as he reported for work. Dr. Travis walked into a raging fire of sickness and death, and he was well prepared for it. On one of their short WhatsApp calls, he told Honora, "It is definitely a virus. It attacks the lungs and doesn't let go. Except for the convalescent plasma treatments that I wrote about, there is no cure or treatment yet."

A few weeks later, governments in many countries, including France, began to shut down all public and private schools, stores, and other establishments except for those deemed "essential" for survival.

They will soon begin shutting down restaurants. And ours will have to close. But for how long? What will happen to us? What will happen to the world? And my baby? Honora lay in bed at night thinking about so many eventualities. For the first time in her life, she started to say her nightly prayers. Honora was seeing a certain pattern or design to her life that started to form when she failed le Bac for the second time. She knew Divine Providence had brought her through so many ups and downs. Her spirit became stronger as time went by, and praying seemed to help. She was responsible for the innocent life inside her now and had to carefully plan for the future. For their future.

Not to worry. The farm is a safe place to be for me, Baby, and Grand-père. But I must find a doctor to make sure everything is okay in there. I can't hide it any longer. Some of the women have figured it out by now. Sometimes Honora felt that she was a spectator in her own life. So much was happening so quickly. But her thoughts and ideas were sound, and she felt that she was doing the right thing for herself and her family.

Sure enough, by the end of March 2020, the authorities had ordered all bars and restaurants in France to shut down indefinitely. Honora had been without a job since the shutdown went into effect. Worse, the French government also restricted all movement of private citizens except for travel for work purposes or emergencies. Everyone had to leave their home with a signed, completed affidavit explaining why and how long they would be outside their homes. It was a forced, national quarantine. The authorities in Paris who decided such things called it a "confinement."

But to those in Normandy, it was much worse than confinement. To those strong, independent, stubborn Viking people, it was imprisonment. Personal liberties were suspended. The now-exploding pandemic had brought about a kind of martial law in France and other countries. Children, pets, women, and men were locked inside their homes or apartments with nowhere to go and with a dwindling food supply, especially in the large cities. It was said that you could get sick just from drinking tap water. Fear controlled and directed humanity now—and nobody knew how long it would last.

Honora heard Normandy locals talk about the virus being like the World War II German occupation— an existence full of dread, danger, and confinement. She was keenly aware of her likeness to these people. She came from their stock. Their strong Viking instincts for survival told them that rural communities where the populations were sparse and spread out had the lowest rate of infections. Not as many of them were going to die. Even better, Normandy's overwhelming agricultural economy meant food would not be a problem. Not like in the cities. Country people ate what they cultivated in their fields, pastures, or backyards and drank clean, fresh, cool water from their deep wells or the sparkling rivers and streams all around them.

Thankfully, the Riaux clan of farmers had complete freedom of movement for conducting their "essential" business. The business of growing and distributing food was more urgent than ever during the pandemic. Honora was always worried about Grand-père exerting himself. Since escaping from the Rouen hospital, the old man didn't let up. He kept his work schedule from pre-dawn to dark, six days a week. He was his own master and had decided that only God would stop him from working his fields. Now that the restaurant was closed, Honora insisted on following Grand-père out to work. Whether he was out directing the combines and loaders, tending the cattle or driving one of the telescopic tractors, she was close by, watching him and dreading that he would have another heart emergency or worse.

Maurice Riaux was a proud old man and did not appreciate being tracked and watched by his granddaughter. To make her useful while she followed him around, Maurice taught his fancy granddaughter how to drive the newest addition to his fleet: the New Holland Boomer 55 HP. The pressure on farmers to produce food was enormous since the government imposed the national quarantine; Eric, Bruno, Maurice, and their regular drivers just couldn't handle the work. Honora was a natural at tractor driving and actually enjoyed it.

She was sure that Grand-père did not know about the baby; she was careful to wear a heavy sweater or jacket to conceal her changing body. But Honora knew the time was quickly approaching when she would have to tell the whole family about her pregnancy. Sometimes, she wondered what had become of Philippe and whether he would even care about their child. The time of reckoning would arrive sooner than she thought.

One day, Honora had to work the Riaux field across the road from the Chateau de Aptot. It brought back so many bittersweet memories to see the old place where Philippe was living when he had tracked her down with the Comtesse at the Riaux farm. It was nearly dark when Honora's tractor finished tilling the Aptot field, and Honora had to climb down from the high cab to shut the big metal gate. The tractor engine was running, but she put the gear in neutral and set the hand brake. The metal steps on the tractor were covered in mud, and Honora's left heel slipped on the final step coming down. Her tight grip on the cab door broke her fall, but her ankle gave way beneath her weight, and it hurt.

She was trying to climb back into the tractor cab when she saw the old châtelaine walk out the chateau's grand portail followed by her groundskeeper. "Honora, c'est vous? Est-ce que vous êtes blessé?" The Comtesse d'Osmoy squinted to see whether it was really Honora and whether she was hurt. The groundskeeper pointed his big spotlight on the tractor and the injured driver, now able to stand.

Honora was surprised and somewhat embarrassed that the lady saw her in such a state. "Bonsoir, Comtesse. It was only a small slip coming down. Nothing serious. You are kind to come out." With that, Honora hastened to get back into the cab and drive away. As quickly as possible. She wondered whether the wise old lady had noticed.

Old age has a way of bestowing a mystical type of wisdom or sixth sense. Women past a certain age who have traversed the many rivers of life and are conscious of their spiritual side often exhibit this inexplicable trait. The Comtesse d'Osmoy slowly walked back into her Chateau after watching Honora drive away in the tractor. She deliberated whether she should make the call to Paris at this late hour or wait until morning. She had not spoken to her widowed cousin, Isabelle Amelia, since the suicide. In the end, the old châtelaine decided: I'll sleep better if I get this call over with tonight.

Honora had gotten used to being awakened by le petit. Her little one, as she called it, had developed a life rhythm, awakening when the light came through Honora's bedroom curtains and sleeping when darkness fell. After all, she estimated that her pregnancy was at least well into its second trimester. She mentally castigated herself for not finding an obstetrician before now. But in Normandy, she had no women to confide in. Then events overtook Honora. A little spotting was on her nightgown the morning after the tractor fall, although she could feel the baby moving as usual. She couldn't procrastinate any further.

"*Bonjour Sandrine, c'est moi, Honora.* Please don't be too shocked. I wanted to tell you before now, but time got away from me. I need to see a good obstetrician right away. I think I'm about twenty weeks pregnant. Don't worry, I feel good, and I think the baby is healthy. But I must see a doctor very soon, today if possible. You are the only person that I have told so far. This is not to be repeated to anyone."

Honora knew that she could count on her close friend. True, lasting friendships were rare; however, the bond between the two young women was such a friendship. Solid, trusting, and never questioning or judging each other. In an instant, Sandrine said, "Of course, I know the perfect doctor for you! She is the top in obstetrics at the American Hospital of Paris. I have her cell phone number and will make the arrangements for you as soon as possible. B*isous Honora, à bientôt.*" Honora was too flustered to question just how her friend came to be acquainted with this baby doctor or why Sandrine possessed the doctor's personal cell phone number.

"Maman, bonjour. I have a few things to do in Paris today. Is there room to park my Land Rover in the garage when I get to the apartment? May I use my old bedroom for one night?" When she answered her daughter's phone call, Chantal Favre had just finished a heated exchange through a Zoom video chat with a tribunal judge over her denied motion. Courtroom battles continued despite the pandemic and nearly everything being shut down. She was pleased to hear from Honora. "*Mai oui, chérie, bien sûr!* Your father will be so happy to see you at home this evening. What a lovely surprise that you are coming to Paris."

The traffic to Paris on the A13 was unusually light that morning. Honora scribbled a quick note to Grand-père about going home to Paris for a couple of days and left the note on the kitchen table where he was sure to see it when he returned that evening. Neuilly-sur-Seine was an elegant, peaceful residential quarter to the northwest of Paris, across the Seine. It was actually a very modern suburb directly adjacent to Paris inhabited mostly by prosperous residents with young families. It was hard to discern the exact point where Paris ended and Neuilly began, unless you lived there.

Neuilly was not only a suburb of Paris but also was a hub for private schools and important medical institutions. One of these was founded by Americans more than a century before Honora's first visit. Seeing the urgent need for medical treatment of American expatriates living in Paris in 1904, a group of visionary doctors and philanthropists founded the American Hospital Association of Paris. A few years later, with generous donations from USA supporters, the association paid cash for a large parcel of land at a high elevation in the center of what was to become the chic suburb of Neilly-sur-Seine. It became world famous and was known as the American Hospital of Paris. It was not an ordinary hospital with ordinary doctors, by any means. Ernest Hemingway, being himself a patriotic American, fired shots at the retreating German forces to defend the American Hospital during the liberation of Paris in 1944.

Records show that prior to 1944 during the Nazi occupation of France, the American Hospital was part of an underground railroad which sheltered, treated, and smuggled wounded Allied soldiers across enemy lines to return to safety and to active duty. Its charitable Foundation, based in New York City, was among the most well-endowed medical non-profits in recent history. With standards of patient care monitored by the American Medical Association, the American Hospital exploded with patients from France and other countries and employed the best qualified, English- speaking physicians of various specialties.

When Honora drove up the hill through the entrance gate of the American Hospital, she was approaching one of the most prestigious and advanced private medical institutions in the world.

Dr. Ursula Hartmann held medical degrees from Munich University and the Grossman School of Medicine at New York University. She had a stellar residency in obstetrics at New York Presbyterian Hospital and devoted most of her waking moments to treating mothers to be and their unborn. Honora could not have been in better hands.

Nevertheless, she was nervous and tensed up when she got into the stirrups and saw the instruments to probe inside her. Dr. Hartmann's physical exam was extremely thorough, to say the least. After the examination, Dr. Hartmann kept her usual clinical composure as Honora answered various questions pertaining to her medical history and pregnancy. But inside, Dr. Hartmann was appalled that this intelligent, well-educated young woman waited so long to seek a doctor's care for herself and her child.

After filling seven blood vials for lab analysis, Dr. Hartmann spoke frankly with Honora. "You waited much too long to get medical attention, although you are now under the best care available in Europe. Fortunately, I see nothing abnormal with your pregnancy, which is at about twenty weeks. The light spotting from this morning is not out of the ordinary at your stage. But we will have to watch it. The lab results will give us a more complete picture. Your baby is very active now, developing quickly. Your body is strong and appears to be very healthy. You will receive a call from my nurse tomorrow after I review the lab results. The blood samples taken include those from your child, which will be screened for congenital abnormalities. The results will also reveal the gender of the fetus."

Honora felt reassured after seeing Dr. Hartmann. She knew that she was in good hands, come what may. It was after 7 p.m. when she drove out of the hospital parking lot. This would be the biggest shock that Honora had ever given Maman and Papa. Or so she thought.

There were plenty of parking slots available in the apartment building on the rue de Constantine. The Land Rover slid right next to the polished, graphite

Peugeot 5008, Jacques Favre's vehicle. She did not use the elevator to go up; the stairs were a welcome exercise for Honora, especially after Dr. Hartmann's positive evaluation. It felt strange to Honora to be turning her key in the big, brass door lock. She had forgotten the comforting aura of entering the huge family apartment; it had been her first home, her original sanctuary. Her pregnant belly was conspicuous now, so her parents were going to immediately know the purpose of her visit. What she faced inside was totally unexpected.

Chantal Favre was prepared. "Bonjour belle! We are so happy to have you back home, even if only for one night. Did you finish doing all your errands? Darling, some people are here to see you. Papa thought it was only proper to receive them while you were in town. We are so excited about our first grandchild!"

Honora went mute. She couldn't even manage a bonsoir. But Isabelle Amelie, Duchesse d'Orléans, took two steps toward Honora and said, *"Enchanté, Honora, je suis la maman de Philippe, je suis ravis de faire votre connaissance."* Those words broke the ice, and Honora responded with a forced smile and small curtsy to the Duchesse.

Never in one million years did Jacques Antoine Favre, respected and feared Paris avocat à la Cour, expect to find himself in a mess like this. His daughter, his only child, was pregnant and unmarried. The runaway father of the baby was standing in his salon with his mother, who happened to be a royal duchess of France and whose dead husband was reputed to be a pervert and Nazi aficionado. But Maître Favre rose to the occasion. He put his arm around his daughter and led her to one of the fauteuils to sit down.

Standing in the middle of the salon, he said, "Honora, you must know why the Duchesse is here with Philippe. We have a right to know what is happening to you and if it involves Philippe. Your mother and I are very concerned." The moment of truth was at hand and the facts spilled out. Jacques and Chantal had been contacted days before by the Duchesse. Her cousin, the Comtesse d'Osmoy, had encountered Honora at Aptot after Honora had a minor accident driving a tractor. She observed certain things about Honora and thought it was high time that Philippe come out of hiding to face his responsibilities.

Philippe remained standing throughout the confrontation with a forlorn expression, his shoulders slumped. His skin had a distinct pallor, like someone committed to an institution. He waited for Honora's father to finish speaking before he said, "Honora, what I have done, running away from you, is unforgivable. What happened to my father devastated me. I was so ashamed of my family and myself. I began to live in mortal fear that I would end up like him. It made me a paranoid and a recluse. My psychiatrist says that I am suffering from a type of PTSD or post-traumatic stress disorder. He is helping me get back my bearings and put this thing behind me. You are the best thing that ever happened to me. I still love you, and I know that you are carrying my child. If you will allow me, I want to try to be a good father to our baby. And I beg your forgiveness."

Honora had been waiting for months to hear these words from Philippe. She had scoured the vast reaches of Normandy searching for him, worrying about him, obsessing over him. But now, she was a different woman. The lovesick, naïve girl that fell madly, abjectly in love with Philippe no longer existed. In her place was a self-assured, decisive, successful woman with her own plan and her own resources to carry it out.

She slowly stood from the fauteuil and, looking at Philippe and his mother, said, "You are both very kind to come here. Of course, Philippe can be a father to our child. I want the best life possible for our baby. Philippe: I forgive you and will always love you. But our relationship ended when you walked out that December day before Christmas. It's impossible to start over. I hope you will regain some semblance of your past life and return to your career at Vinci. But the Honora that you loved is no longer here." Then, Chantal and Jacques Favre watched their daughter calmly walk out of their salon and close the door behind her, leaving Philippe and his mother speechless.

Chapter 12

The Circle

It was wonderful to return to Paris and to the Cabinet Favre. Honora was asked to return by her father. After witnessing her success managing Eric's restaurant at La Bec-Hellouin, Jacques Favre was convinced that Honora was more than capable of running the administrative side of his law firm's operations. There was never any question that she would stay at the family apartment where she grew up, and she wanted le petit to come into the world via the American Hospital of Paris under the care of Dr. Hartmann.

Honora and Philippe were having a son; the expected due date was in late August 2020. It was a foregone conclusion that the boy would carry his father's name and inherit his titles and honors, the same Philippe had received from his father, the Duc d'Orléans. Honora kept Philippe's mother, the Duchesse, updated on the baby's progress and plans for the birth. It was still too painful to connect directly with Philippe.

France was still under a confinement or quarantine order, but the cabinet continued working on client cases online. Zoom video conferences with lawyers and clients became the norm for doing business, and the law firm's profits were holding steady in 2020. Honora had been the administrative director of the Cabinet Favre since June. She felt a strange, almost morbid sensation stepping into the shoes of Madame Paul, who had met a most gruesome torture and death, likely at the hands of her drug cartel partners. But she kept extremely busy at the apartment overlooking Napoléon's Tomb and the magnificent Esplanade gardens.

Relocating several of the commercial-sized desktop computers, worktables, files, and supplies from the cabinet offices to Chantal's elegant salon, Honora transformed it into a command center for all legal work produced by the various lawyers. The fine antiques and her mother's cherished silk canapés were carefully covered in sheets and pushed against the walls of fine boiseries. Her parents were incredulous that their young daughter now successfully coordinated business operations remotely with each of the Favre staff attorneys who kept producing billable client hours from their homes. It was a feat of desperation and inspiration. The Favre law business was not "confined" or shut down by the pandemic. On the contrary, it prospered during hard times.

Despite his intense work schedule, Kevin insisted that they see each other on WhatsApp at least once each week. The language barrier between them had somehow vanished, and they spoke to each other in a funny, romantic jumble of English and French. In their last visit, he told her he was seeing light at the end of the tunnel for the pandemic, although it was expected that the death toll would reach one million before the end of the summer months.

Dr. Travis was now assistant chief of virology at the Methodist Research Institute. Because of his published work on convalescent plasma therapy, he was pulled into the inner circle of virology and vaccine experts organized by President Trump months before. It was called Operation Warp Speed.

Its sole task was to develop, test, and obtain government approval for the first-ever vaccine that would protect people against the mysterious contagion. Their deadline was "immediately" and no later than year-end 2020. It was a race by the top pharmaceutical conglomerates in the world to save humanity; a vaccine of this magnitude had never been created in less than five years. The media and traditional virology experts fully expected Operation Warp Speed to fail and never hesitated to publicly express their negative, defeatist opinions. But Dr. Travis and the others working on Warp Speed knew better.

Despite the distance between them and the turmoil around them, the unlikely couple was more in love than ever. Tragedy and uncertainty had united them. Honora longed for a time when the world was back to normal, and she could board an Air France direct flight from Paris Charles de Gaulle airport to Houston's George Bush Intercontinental with *le petit garçon*. They loved debating whether to have their wedding in Paris or Houston and how the logistics would work. She was excited about living in America as the wife of a successful, highly respected physician. Her little boy, of course, would grow up bilingual and bicultural.

She reached the pinnacle of her stellar career with the Christine Paul investigation. For the past seven months, Yasmine LaGarde had led more than a dozen INTERPOL agents searching, interrogating, and tracking down cartel bosses, runners, and mercenaries that the notorious Christine Paul had organized and coordinated in running a multi-billion-euro business. When she was murdered, Paul was the acting CEO of a hugely successful organization engaged in buying, importing, and distributing opiates and crack cocaine in Europe's largest metropolitan centers.

Detective LaGarde braced herself for the arrest she was about to make at no. 11 rue de Constantine. INTERPOL had obtained signed witness statements that the man about to be detained was, in fact, the mastermind behind the web of cartels managed by Paul. Jacques Favre had been most gracious and cooperative when LaGarde had questioned him last December following the death of his long-time, trusted employee. At the time, he appeared perfectly innocent. LaGarde's investigation had proven otherwise.

"Bonjour, c'est Detective LaGarde. Can you please buzz us in? We are here to see attorney Jacques Favre." Her voice was quite calm and business-like, and she was accompanied by two armed officers from the prefecture of Paris, although Honora, who answered the door buzzer, couldn't see them. It was Honora's father who opened the front door to the apartment. Jacques had just finished a conference call in his study and was dressed in his normal office attire, a dark business suit with an immaculately laundered white shirt and Hermès tie. Nothing could have been further from his mind than what happened next.

"Monsieur, we have a warrant for your detention in connection with the activities attributed to your former employee, Christine Paul. If you accompany us voluntarily, there will be no need for handcuffs." He felt the blood drain from his face and had trouble taking a normal breath. But Jacques Favre acknowledged what Detective LaGarde said and replied, "Very well, I will accompany you. Before taking me, allow me to speak to my daughter. She is in the next room."

Honora had already come out of her salon/ command center to listen to the detective, and she approached her father, who was in the foyer with the officers. *"T'inquiète pas*, Papa. I will find Maman, and she will know how to proceed. I'm sure that she will come to you very quickly."

Seconds after Jacques Favre was escorted into the police vehicle with LaGarde, Honora received a call from her mother. Chantal was already at the prefecture of Paris with a criminal law specialist who would be defending Jacques. She had been on official business with a client and had received a tip from a friend at the prefecture that Jacques was going to be arrested at their home, imminently.

It was reported that INTERPOL had witness statements tying him to drug cartel crimes. A man named Youssef swore he knew and regularly took orders from Christine Paul and Jacques Favre to carry out drug shipments to Marseille and Munich. Chantal's grapevine at the prefecture and INTERPOL further whispered that the famous criminal defense lawyer, Simon Weisz, was representing Youssef.

At a chargeable rate of one thousand euros per hour, everybody understood that Weisz was not simply "Youssef's lawyer." Weisz was actually retained and paid by a third party with unlimited resources, most likely Youssef's real bosses in the cartels. Worse, Weisz was known and feared by the prefecture and prosecutors for cleverly crafting loopholes or technical fault lines in charges against his criminal clients, thereby forcing the charging authorities to accept a generous plea bargain with his client. It was suspected that the "witness statements" against Honora's father had come from this kind of dirty deal. A quid pro quo between the criminal and the prosecutors.

Yasmine LaGarde hated this part of her job. Negotiating with the drug cartels to try to make more arrests, quite possibly of innocent people who were mere bystanders in the criminal enterprise. But she had no choice. It was the system in which she had to work and succeed to keep scaling the INTERPOL hierarchy.

Within minutes, Honora was bombarded with dozens of emails and text messages from the cabinet's staff and lawyers about her father's arrest. The Favres and their battalion of staff lawyers had long tentacles and several highly placed "friends" in law enforcement. Most couldn't and wouldn't believe that Jacques Favre was guilty of such crimes.

Feeling like a general walking into battle, Honora sat down at one of the desktops in her command center and whipped out an official press release written on the law firm's formal letterhead "Cabinet Favre, No. 15 Avenue d'Iéna, 75116 Paris." The announcement went out via email to more than five thousand clients and former clients, professional lawyer's associations, and all Paris, New York, London, and Dubai media outlets. It was brief but to the point.

Cabinet Favre
No. 15 Avenue d'Iéna
75116 Paris

Today, the co-founder and senior partner of the cabinet, Maître Jacques Antoine Favre, was detained for questioning by law enforcement authorities. He is fully cooperating with their investigation, and it is expected that he soon will be cleared of all wrongdoing and return to his law practice. In the meantime, Attorney Chantal Louise Favre, a cabinet co-founder and senior partner, and Mademoiselle Honora Blanche Favre, administrative director, together with all other attorneys employed at the firm, will continue to conduct normal operations of the cabinet without interruption and without prejudice to our client's interests. Thank you for your understanding and loyalty.

Honora Blanche Favre
Paris
2 July 2020

The circle was now complete for Honora. Life had carried her, successfully, through a rushing river of experiences, good and bad, to reach this day, and she was right back where she started years ago as a frightened schoolgirl. She made the full circle back to Paris with courage, tenacity, and most of all with an unfettered belief in herself. *We will get through this, and Papa will be free and respected again. It's just one more thing to face and resolve. But I could never be doing this today if I had not learned so much in Normandy. So many depend on me now; I won't let them down.* Honora felt her petit garçon move inside her as these thoughts ran through her mind. Her feminine force had never been never stronger.

About the Author

Linda F. Barrett is an international lawyer, historian, and a Texas native. Her work has taken her around the world for more than 40 years. She is fluent in English, Spanish and French.

A life-long philanthropist and animal lover, Linda founded the Houston BARC Foundation in 2010, which, with the support and guidance of city elected leaders, permanently transformed the way stray animals are treated, saved, and adopted at Houston's municipal facilities.

Linda and her husband are dedicated to restoring historical monuments in Normandy, France and to raising awareness of the close historical and cultural bonds between the United States and Western European countries.

web: LindaFBarrett.com
X: @HonoraBarrett

www.ingramcontent.com/pod-product-compliance
Lightning Source LLC
Chambersburg PA
CBHW070507200726

48293CB00007B/2421